TO AVOID OVERDUE CHARGES THIS BOOK SHOULD BE
RETURNED ON OR BEFORE THE LAST DATE STAMPED
ABOVE. IF NOT REQUIRED BY ANOTHER READER IT MAY
BE RENEWED BY PERSONAL CALL, TELEPHONE OR POST.

24/6/10

18 AUG 2010

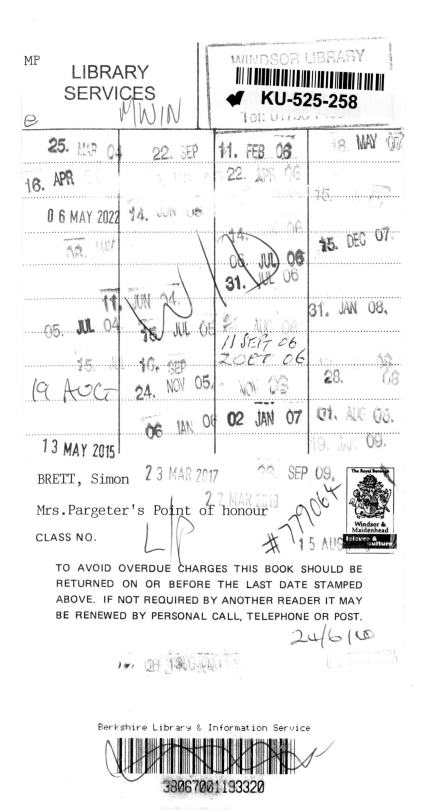

MRS PARGETER'S POINT OF HONOUR

When Mrs Pargeter is asked by an elderly widow to return a large number of stolen paintings to their rightful owners, she doesn't hesitate for it's a point of honour to complete any of her late husband's unfinished business. So she contacts Truffler Mason, Hedgeclipper Clinton and others of the late Mr Pargeter's associates to sort out the operation. But all does not run smoothly, because Detective Inspector Craig Wilkinson, still embittered by his failure to arrest Mr Pargeter while he was alive, starts to show an unhealthy interest in the man's widow ...

To Corinne

Mrs Pargeter's Point Of Honour

by
Simon Brett

Magna Large Print Books
Long Preston, North Yorkshire,
England.

British Library Cataloguing in Publication Data.

Brett, Simon
Mrs Pargeter's point of honour.

A catalogue record for this book is
available from the British Library

ISBN 0-7505-1394-2

First published in Great Britain by Macmillan, an imprint of
Macmillan Publishers Ltd., 1998

Published in Large Print 1999 by arrangement with Macmillan
Publishers Ltd.

Magna Large Print is an imprint of
Library Magna Books Ltd.
Printed and bound in Great Britain by
T.J. International Ltd., Cornwall, PL28 8RW.

Chapter One

Gary the chauffeur whistled, as the spiked gates opened automatically. 'Bennie Logan done all right for himself, didn't he, Mrs Pargeter?'

'Yes,' the plump, white-haired lady in the back of the limousine agreed. 'Pity he didn't live longer to enjoy it.'

What Bennie Logan didn't live longer to enjoy was the Elizabethan manor house up whose drive they were proceeding at an appropriately decorous pace. The exceptionally warm September afternoon showed the building at its best. Chastaigne Varleigh was a monument to elegance in discreetly mellowed red brick, punctuated here and there by fine leaded windows. It had been sympathetically restored to its earlier magnificence, and the surrounding grounds showed the same punctilious attention to cosmetic detail. No mole would have dared to break through the even green of the lawns, no weed would have had the effrontery to poke up through

5

the valeted gravel that led to the front door of Chastaigne Varleigh.

Mrs Pargeter's pull on the chain of the doorbell was answered by Veronica Chastaigne. What the house's owner saw on her doorstep was a well-upholstered woman in a bright silk print dress. The visitor had beautifully cut white hair, and her body tapered down to surprisingly elegant ankles and surprisingly high-heeled shoes. There was about the woman an aura of comfort and ease. Though this was their first encounter, Veronica Chastaigne felt as if they had met before, and as if here was someone in whom she would have no difficulty in confiding anything.

The house's interior reflected the same care and discreet opulence as its exterior. The sitting room into which Veronica Chastaigne ushered her guest was oak-panelled, but prevented from being gloomy by the bright prints which upholstered its sofas and armchairs. Sunlight, beaming through the tall leaded windows, enriched their glow. The room had nothing to prove; it manifested the casual ease of the genuine aristocrat, to whom such surroundings were nothing unusual.

And Veronica Chastaigne looked as if

she had lived in them from birth. Though now nearly eighty, she still had a majesty in her gaunt features, an ancestral hauteur in the long bony fingers that handled the silver and fine china of the coffee tray. But she quickly disabused her guest of the notion that she had always lived in the house.

'Oh, no,' her effortlessly patrician vowels pronounced. 'Bennie changed our surname to Chastaigne when we bought the place.'

Mrs Pargeter looked appropriately surprised. 'I'd assumed Chastaigne Varleigh had been in your family for generations.'

The older woman chuckled. 'I'm afraid nothing stayed in my family for very long—estates, paintings, jewellery—it all had to be sold off eventually. We were the original titled spendthrifts. Bennie was the one who accumulated things.'

She then showed Mrs Pargeter some of the 'things' that her late husband had 'accumulated'. They were hung in a panelled Long Gallery which ran the length of the third floor of the house, and some of them were very old 'things' indeed. Old Masters, in fact. Though Mrs Pargeter had no formal training in art, she could recognize the translucence of a Giotto, the russet hues of a Rembrandt, the softened shadows of a Leonardo. And, coming more up to date, she had no difficulty identifying the haziness of Turner, the geometry of Mondrian, the tortured whorls of Van Gogh. (In artistic appreciation, she had always followed the precept of the late Mr Pargeter: 'I don't know much about art, but I know what it's worth.')

'They're quite magnificent,' she breathed to her hostess in awestruck tones.

'Yes, not bad, are they?' Veronica agreed briskly.

Then came the innocent enquiry, 'Do you open the gallery to the public, Mrs Chastaigne?'

The elderly aristocrat got as near to blushing as her upbringing would allow. 'No, I don't think that would be quite the thing.' In response to an interrogative stare, she continued, 'You see, my dear, all of these paintings are ... in the terminology of the criminal fraternity ... hot.'

Mrs Pargeter nodded comfortably. 'Oh. I see.'

It was after six o'clock when they returned to the sitting room. 'Certainly time for sherry,' Veronica Chastaigne announced in a tone which admitted no possibility of disagreement.

Not that Mrs Pargeter would have disagreed, anyway. She was of the belief that there were quite enough unpleasant things in life, and that it was therefore the duty of the individual to indulge in the pleasant ones at every opportunity. She raised her crystal glass of fine Amontillado to catch the rays of the September evening sun.

'Cheers,' she said, waiting patiently for the information which she knew must come. Veronica Chastaigne had invited her to Chastaigne Varleigh for a purpose. Soon she would discover what that purpose was.

But the old lady was in nostalgic mood, caught in bitter-sweet reminiscence of her late husband. 'No woman could have asked for a more considerate companion than Bennie. Or more loving. The moment he first burst on to my horizon when I was twenty-one years old, I was totally bowled over. I'd never met anyone like him.'

'Oh?' Mrs Pargeter knew to a nicety how minimal the prompts to confidence needed to be.

Veronica chuckled. 'Could have come from another planet. You see, up to that point my social life had all been the "season" and hunt balls. I'd been surrounded by chinless wonders. People of "our own sort". The "right class of person".'

'So your parents didn't approve of Bennie?'

'Hardly. They were absolutely appalled. Mind you, I was far better off with him than I would have been with any of the titled peabrains they were offering. And the day we were married, Bennie promised that he would keep me in the lifestyle to which I was accustomed.'

'Hence Chastaigne Varleigh?'

'Yes. And, er, the pictures.' The old lady gave a sweet and innocent smile. 'I never thought it proper to enquire into the sources of my husband's wealth.'

'Very wise.' Mrs Pargeter had had a similar arrangement with the late Mr Pargeter.

'Shortly before Bennie died ...' Veronica Chastaigne spoke more slowly as she approached the real purpose of their encounter, 'he assured me that, if ever I needed any assistance ... assistance, that is, in matters where an approach to the police would not have been the appropriate course of action ...'

Mrs Pargeter nodded. She knew exactly what the older woman meant.

'... I should contact his "good mate", Mr Pargeter.' She focused faded blue eyes on her guest. 'I was therefore not a little surprised when my summons was answered by you rather than by your husband.'

'I'm sorry to say that Mr Pargeter is also ... no longer with us.'

'Ah.'

'Dead,' Mrs Pargeter amplified readily.

'I understood the first time.' Veronica Chastaigne's face became thoughtful, and even a little disappointed. 'Mmm. So perhaps I will have to look elsewhere for assistance ...'

'Don't you believe it,' Mrs Pargeter hastened to reassure her. 'I regard it as a point of honour to discharge all of my husband's unfinished business.'

This news brought a sparkle back to the old lady's eye. Her guest leant enthusiastically forward in her armchair. 'So tell me—what is it needs doing?'

There was only a moment's hesitation before Veronica Chastaigne also leant forward and began to share the problem that had caused her to summon Mrs Pargeter to Chastaigne Varleigh.

Chapter Two

A silver open-topped Porsche was approaching the automatic gates of Chastaigne Varleigh as Gary's limousine, with Mrs Pargeter tucked neatly in the back, swept out of the drive. The Porsche was driven by a man of about forty, dark-haired, good-looking, but beginning to run to fat.

He watched the departing limousine with curiosity tinged with suspicion before surging up the drive to the old house in an incautious flurry of gravel.

The Porsche's driver entered the sitting room, gave Veronica Chastaigne a functional peck on the forehead and an 'Evening, Mother,' before crossing to pour himself a large whisky.

She shook herself out of a wistful daze to greet her son. 'Hello, Toby dear.'

'Who was that driving off in the limo?' he asked casually.

The faded blue eyes grew vague. 'What? Oh, just someone about the Guide Dogs for the Blind Bring-and-Buy.'

'Ah,' said Toby, as if that settled the matter.

But his dark eyes, sinking in rolls of fat, flashed a suspicious look at his mother. He didn't believe her.

Veronica's son wasn't the only one with suspicions about Chastaigne Varleigh. Had Toby known it, the arrival of his Porsche had been observed through binoculars from an unmarked car parked at a local beauty spot which overlooked the estate. The same binoculars had also registered the arrival and departure of Gary's limousine. And these comings and goings had been noted down on a clipboard by the passenger next to the man with the binoculars.

'Patience is probably the most important quality in a good copper, certainly in a good detective,' said Detective Inspector Craig Wilkinson, tapping the ash of his cigarette out of the open slot at the top of his window. 'Patience and timing.'

'Yes,' said Detective Sergeant Hughes, not for the first time that day. He found that being with the DI involved saying 'yes' a lot. Not that the Sergeant regarded himself as a yesman. By no means. When

13

the moment came he would assert himself, he had no doubt of that. Nor did he have any doubt about his exceptional skills as a policeman.

But he'd only just been made up to detective sergeant and transferred down from Sheffield; this day's surveillance with Inspector Wilkinson was his first in his new status; so deference to superior experience was clearly in order. But Hughes didn't plan that the situation should stay that way for long. This job with the Met was going to be a new start for him. He'd abandoned the girlfriend he'd been living with for the previous four years; he didn't want any hangovers from his Sheffield life to slow down the advance of his career in London. Hughes was a bright, ambitious young man, and he was in a hurry to have his brightness recognized and his ambition realized.

'Oh no, softly, softly catchee monkey,' the Inspector went on. 'When you've been in the Police Force as long as I have, you'll find that's the only method that really pays off in the long term. Though I dare say at times, to a youngster like you, that approach could seem pretty boring.'

'Yes,' said Sergeant Hughes, with rather

more feeling than on the previous occasions. They had been sitting for four hours watching Chastaigne Varleigh; so far all they'd seen had been the arrival and departure of the limo and the arrival of the Porsche. To compound the pointlessness of the exercise, at the moment of Mrs Pargeter's emergence from Gary's limousine, Inspector Wilkinson had had his binoculars lowered while he pontificated about the number of years it took to make a good copper and how there were no short cuts possible in the process. Since he'd also managed to miss her coming out of the mansion, Wilkinson had no idea what Veronica Chastaigne's visitor looked like. It was only at the insistence of Sergeant Hughes that they'd made a note of the limousine's registration number.

To add to the serious doubts he was beginning to entertain about his superior's competence, Hughes, a non-smoker and something of a fitness fanatic, was not enjoying the acrid fug that had been building up in the car. He knew that when he took them off in his flat that evening, his clothes would still smell of tobacco smoke.

Inspector Wilkinson's ruminative monologue continued. 'No, you have to plan, look ahead, build up your case slowly, and then, when everything's ready, double-checked and sorted, you have to—*move in like lightning!*'

'Yes,' said Sergeant Hughes, who by now had an instinct for the length of pause that required filling.

'Hmm ...' His boss nodded thoughtfully. Inspector Wilkinson was a large, craggy man, only a few years off retirement. He had all the standard accoutrements for someone in his position—a divorce and a variety of subsequent messy relationships, an expression of permanent disappointment, a thin grey moustache, and an antagonistic attitude to his immediate superior, whom he regarded as a 'jumped-up, university-educated, pen-pushing desk-driver'.

Wilkinson was not close to any of his professional colleagues. He had always hoped that at some stage in his career he would be paired up on a regular basis with a congenial young copper, with whom he could build up an ongoing mutually insulting but ultimately affectionate rela-tionship. However, it hadn't happened yet, and from what he'd seen of his latest sidekick, wasn't about to happen.

Wilkinson had been an Inspector for longer than most people at the station could remember. He had been passed over so often for higher promotions that now he no longer even bothered to fill in the application forms. But that did not mean he was without ambition. Once before in his career, he had been very close to making a major coup, bringing an entire criminal network to justice. For logistical reasons, things hadn't worked out on that occasion, but now he felt he was close to another triumph on a comparable scale. And this time nothing was going to screw it up.

Inspector Wilkinson looked at his watch. Like all his movements, the raising of his arm, the turn of his wrist to show the time, was slow and deliberate. Sergeant Hughes already knew that if the two of them had to spend a lot of time together, he would very quickly get infuriated by these slow, deliberate movements.

'Another forty-two minutes and we can have another cup of coffee from the thermos,' said Inspector Wilkinson. Then, generously, 'You can have another cup of mine, Hughes.'

'Thank you, sir.'

'But another day, be a good idea to bring your own thermos. Always be as independent of other people as you can. That's another mark of a good copper.'

'I'll bring my own next time,' the Sergeant mumbled.

'Be best. Of course you have to plan your coffee intake when you're on a stake-out. Don't want to be needing a widdle at that vital moment when you have to—*move in like lightning!* Do you?'

'No,' said Sergeant Hughes, welcoming the variety. Then, emboldened by the change of monosyllable, he ventured a question. 'Can you tell me a bit more about why we're actually doing this stake-out, sir?'

'Well, I *could*,' the Inspector replied, tapping his nose slowly with a forefinger, 'but whether I *will* or not is another matter. When I'm on a case, I always operate on a "need to know" basis, and what I have to ask myself in this instance is: "How much do you need to know?"'

'I'd have thought, the more I knew, the better it would be.'

'In what way?'

'Then we could discuss the information

we have. We could have the benefit of each other's input.'

'*Input?*' Inspector Wilkinson enunciated the word with distaste. 'When I want your input, Hughes, I will ask for it. Anyway, that hasn't really answered my question about how much you need to know.'

'To put it at its most basic,' said the Sergeant with a note of exasperation in his voice, 'if I don't know what we're looking for in this surveillance, then I'm not going to recognize it when I see it, am I?'

'A good answer.' Wilkinson nodded. 'Yes, a good answer—were it not for one small detail. A good copper, you'll find, will always notice that one significant detail in any scenario. Any idea what the detail might be in this case?'

'No,' said the Sergeant, who didn't want to get caught up in elaborate guessing games.

'The detail is that *you're* not looking for anything.' The Inspector tapped his binoculars. '*I* am looking for things and telling you what I see. *You* are simply writing down what I tell you.'

'Yes,' Sergeant Hughes agreed listlessly. He hadn't got the energy to point out that Wilkinson had so far missed the most important detail to have come up during their surveillance. They still had no idea what Veronica Chastaigne's first visitor looked like.

'But I will give you one piece of information relevant to the case ...' the Inspector went on with new magnanimity.

'What?' There was now a spark of animation in the Sergeant's eye.

'It concerns criminals.'

'Oh.' The spark was extinguished. 'Thank you very much, Inspector.'

Back in the big house, Toby Chastaigne was himself involved in surveillance. All the way through their supper he kept a watchful eye on his mother, his anxious scrutiny masked by a veil of solicitude.

'You should eat more,' he said, as he watched her peck at a flake of salmon.

'Why?' Veronica asked abstractedly.

'Build yourself up,' Toby replied, as he reached across to replenish his plate with a mound of buttered new potatoes and dollops of mayonnaise.

'What for?'

Her son looked thoughtful, but decided not to answer this. He let a pause hang between them, then, with over-elaborate casualness, asked, 'Have you done anything about the will yet?' Veronica looked up sharply, as he hastened to soften his bluntness. 'I speak as an accountant, not as your son. This is the advice I'd give to any of my clients. It's just that one has to be practical—one should always have all the loose ends neatly tied up.'

A pale smile came to Veronica Chastaigne's thin lips. 'That could almost be your motto, Toby couldn't it?'

He looked injured by the injustice of her implied slight. 'Mother, I'm only thinking of you.'

'Very kind.' She smiled again, a kindly smile, though neither of them was in any doubt that the conversation was gladiatorial rather than benign. The courtesy was no more than a front. 'Though I don't really see how ...' Veronica went on lightly, 'because loose ends aren't going to worry me too much, are they?'

'Well ...'

'After I'm dead,' she continued easily, 'they'll be someone else's problem.'

Toby coughed in embarrassment, sending a fine spray of potato over his plate. 'I wish you wouldn't talk about it, Mother.'

'Why not?' asked Veronica, enjoying her

son's discomfiture. 'You said you wanted me to be practical. I'd have thought preparing for something you know is going to happen is extremely practical. And my death is certainly going to happen—in the not-too-distant future. You know, your father always used to say—'

Toby raised an admonitory hand. 'I don't want to hear any more criminal maxims, thank you, Mother.'

That really caught her on the raw. The gloves were very definitely off, as she snapped at him, 'Don't try and disclaim your own father, Toby! He worked harder than you've ever worked to provide us with all this.'

'Hard work is not the point at issue,' Toby snapped back. 'It's the nature of his work that was so shameful.'

His words only served to incense his mother further. 'Shameful? Your own father? Bennie did all that work so that you would be able to take the legitimate route through life. Eton, Cambridge, the accountancy training. He gave you everything you now possess, Toby.'

'That is your view, Mother.' The flash of anger had given way to his customary controlled urbanity. 'As you know, I don't share it. I think my current position in life is due at least as much to my own intelligence and application as to anything my father gave me.'

'I see,' said his mother, still seething. 'So you despise the things your father gave you?'

Toby tried to make his tone conciliatory, but he couldn't keep out a little tinge of the patronizing. 'I didn't say that, Mother. It's just ... well, we both know what my father was ... but there doesn't seem to me any need to dwell on it.'

'As you wish.' Veronica Chastaigne sighed, aligned her knife and fork on her plate and pushed the hardly touched remains of her meal towards the centre of the table.

Toby smiled a self-satisfied smile, as though his point had been taken and he had won the round. Leaning forward to fork up another mound of salmon, potatoes and mayonnaise, he could not see the expression on his mother's face. Had he registered its mix of distaste, shrewd calculation and sheer bloody-mindedness, he would have realized that the round was far from won.

In fact, Veronica Chastaigne's face

showed a determination to escalate the conflict with her son into all-out war. And it was not a war that she contemplated the possibility of losing.

Chapter Three

The offices of the Mason De Vere Detective Agency, situated above a betting shop in South London, would have got a very high rating from the Society for the Preservation of Dust. Other organizations—like the Society for the Maintenance of Tidiness, the Association for Efficient Filing or the Commission for the Removal of Encrusted Coffee Cups—might have marked it rather lower. In fact, they would have given it no marks at all.

But, though unlikely to impress potential clients, the office was arranged exactly the way Truffler Mason liked it. Since he was the sole proprietor—the 'De Vere' being merely a fiction to look impressive on a letterhead—he could please himself in such matters. And, though his office might have the musty air of an attic which had lain undisturbed for half a century, inside it he knew exactly where everything was. Every shoebox, fluffy with dust; every overfull and spilling cardboard folder; every pile of frayed brown envelopes, cinched by perished rubber bands; every crumpled clump of yellowed cuttings pinned to the wall; they all meant something to Truffler Mason. Whatever the reference that was required, within seconds and in a minor tornado of dust, he would have the relevant paper in his hand.

Mrs Pargeter had known her late husband's former associate too long to pass comment on—or even to notice—the squalor in which he worked. Anyway, she was not a woman who set much store by outward appearances. She judged people by instinct; on first meeting she saw into their souls and instantly assessed them. Only on a few, painful occasions had her judgement been proved to be at fault.

And one select band of people she approved of even before she met them. These were the group honoured by inclusion in Mrs Pargeter's most treasured heirloom—her husband's address book. The late Mr Pargeter, an adoring and solicitous spouse, had left his widow well-provided for in the financial sense, but from beyond the grave he had also given her a far more valuable protection. In his varied and colourful business career, the late Mr Pargeter had worked with a rich gallery of characters of wide-ranging individual skills, and it was these whose names filled the precious address book. As a result, if ever his widow came up against one of those little niggling challenges which bother us all from time to time—finding a missing person, gaining access to a locked building, removing property without its owner's knowledge, replacing a lost document, or even obtaining one which had had no previous existence—all she had to do was to look up in the book the number of a person with the appropriate skills, and her problem would be instantly resolved. Such was the loyalty inspired by her late husband amongst his workforce that the words on the telephone, 'Hello, this is Mrs Pargeter' prompted immediate shelving of all other work and dedicated concentration on her requirements.

She had worked so often with Truffler Mason that she had almost forgotten he'd had a life before he became a private investigator. But she was gratefully aware of his unrivalled knowledge of criminal behaviour, his proficiency at obtaining information from people, and his encyclopaedic list of contacts when less sophisticated manpower was required. The fact that in learning these skills he had not followed the traditional career path of a detective was something to which Mrs Pargeter never gave a moment's thought.

When Truffler's tall presence came to greet her at the door of his outer office—a space only marginally less dusty than the inner sanctum—she commented on the absence of his secretary Bronwen.

'Ah, yes, she's off for a while,' Truffler Mason intoned, in his customary voice, a deeply tragic rumble which made Eeyore sound as bouncy as Little Noddy.

'Not ill, I hope?'

'No, no, she's got married.'

'Again?' Mrs Pargeter asked doubtfully. She knew that Bronwen's marital history was a catalogue of unsatisfactory skirmishes and pitched battles, that in fact it shared many features with the Hundred Years War.

'Again,' Truffler concurred gloomily. 'Oh yes, I've heard all about it for months. Love's young dream this time. They were meant for each other. They're blissfully happy. This time it's for ever.'

'So are you going to have to hire someone else?'

He shook his huge head. 'No, give it a couple of weeks ... she'll be back.'

From long, but unjudgemental, knowledge of the hygiene standards that obtained in his office, Mrs Pargeter refused Truffler Mason's offer of a cup of coffee, but made no attempt to wipe the dust from the seat towards which he ushered her. He coiled his long body down into his own chair the other side of the desk, and listened intently while she brought him up to date with her visit to Chastaigne Varleigh.

'Mrs Chastaigne is dying, you see, Truffler,' said Mrs Pargeter.

'I'm sorry,' he responded automatically, in a voice more doom-laden than ever.

'No need to be. She's very philosophical about it. Knows that the best bit of her life was while Bennie was alive. Knows that she's had the great privilege of living in comfort surrounded by beautiful things ...'

He nodded. Though Truffler Mason had

never actually been to Chastaigne Varleigh, he'd heard on a secret grapevine of its amazing hidden art collection. 'So what does she want from us, Mrs P?'

She grimaced. 'It's the beautiful things, Truffler …'

'What, all that stuff Bennie Logan nicked for her?'

Mrs Pargeter nodded. 'Right. The paintings. She wants them returned.'

'Returned?'

'Restored to their rightful owners. Every last one of them.'

Truffler Mason let out a low whistle and shook his head in disbelief. 'Blimey O'Reilly,' he muttered.

Chapter Four

'You know, a good copper,' said Inspector Wilkinson, 'is a copper who makes his mark.'

'Really?' On his third day of sitting in an unmarked smoke-filled car with the DI, Sergeant Hughes was beginning to vary his responses. No longer was he content with

29

just the subservient 'yes'; now increasingly he used words that ended with question marks, implying a degree of scepticism, even the blasphemous possibility that he was not accepting everything the Inspector said as gospel truth.

Initially, Hughes had given his boss the benefit of the doubt. Maybe that ponderous manner and apparent stupidity masked a brain of rare brilliance. Maybe the unprepossessing exterior was a smokescreen for a genius of detection.

After two days spent in the man's company, the Sergeant had ruled out both these possibilities. With Inspector Wilkinson, he came to the conclusion, what you saw was what you got. The only smokescreen he was capable of putting up came from his cigarettes.

'Yes,' said Wilkinson.

Maybe it was this transient moment of role reversal that emboldened Hughes to ask a direct question. 'And would you say you have made your mark, sir?'

'Oh, I think people remember me. Yes, though I say it myself, I think Detective Inspector Craig Wilkinson is a name that has a certain resonance in the Met.'

'And for what reason does it resonate?'

Boredom was driving the Sergeant's questions ever closer to the limits of acceptability.

This one, however, prompted another slow finger-tap to the inspectorial nose. 'Bit hush-hush. Mostly for the kind of undercover operations that, by their very nature, can't have too much publicity. But which are deeply appreciated by those few authority figures who're in the know.'

'Oh yes?' Hughes's sceptical intonation was now a million miles from the unquestioning yeses of his first day. 'Would you be referring to the painstaking stalking and capture of criminal masterminds, sir, that sort of thing?'

'That sort of thing,' Inspector Wilkinson confirmed with a knowing nod of the head. 'That sort of thing, yes, young Hughes. Of course, I'd like to tell you more, but we're treading around the kind of delicate area in which one can't be too careful.'

'And is what we're engaged in at the moment another operation that involves the painstaking stalking and will lead to the eventual capture of another criminal mastermind, sir?'

'Shrewd guess, Hughes, shrewd guess.

You are not a million miles from the truth there.'

'I still think it'd help if you told me a bit of detail about the case we're actually investigating at the ...'

But a slow, admonitory finger had risen to Wilkinson's lips and once again the Sergeant's words trickled away into frustrated silence.

'No, no,' said the Inspector. 'A case has to be conducted at the appropriate pace, and information has to be fed out sparingly. A few careless words in the pub, a bit of incautious pillow talk ... those are the kind of things that can ruin months—even years—of punctilious build-up.'

'Yes,' Sergeant Hughes agreed listlessly, his moment of assertiveness past.

Inspector Wilkinson stroked his moustache complacently. It was a sad moustache. An old moustache. A moustache dating from the days when a pencil line along Clark Gable's upper lip was deemed to be sexy. And even for people who liked that kind of thing, the Inspector's moustache was disfigured by being grey—except for a small patch, slightly right of centre, which was yellow from his habit of smoking untipped cigarettes right down to the end.

'No, you'll find that a good copper,' he went on, 'a good copper is aware at all times of the level of security required in a given situation and the degree of information dissemination necessary to—'

'Excuse me, sir. Don't you think that could be the person we're looking for? She looks as if she's going to get into the car.'

The Inspector followed Hughes's pointing finger to see a plump, white-haired woman in a bright red coat stepping daintily across the pavement between the betting-shop entrance and a limousine parked on the double yellow lines directly outside.

'Well spotted, Hughes.' Wilkinson opened his car door.

'Shall I come with you, sir?'

'No, thank you.'

'But I'm the one who found out where we'd find the limousine. I got on to the police computer and—'

'Computers, huh.' Inspector Wilkinson let out a patronizing chuckle. 'Your generation thinks computers can give all the answers. But, you know, they'll never replace the instincts of a good copper.'

'Oh, can't I come with you?' Hughes pleaded pathetically.

'No, no. Subtle approach is what's required at this moment. Don't want to raise any suspicions.'

'About *what?*' asked the Sergeant in a wail of frustration. But the car door had already closed behind his uncommunicative boss.

Mrs Pargeter was settling into the comfortable upholstery of the limousine's back seat when she heard a tap on the window. She pressed a button and the pane slid silently down. Facing her she found the craggy face of a man in his fifties. He had a thin moustache and a cigarette drooped from the corner of his mouth. 'Good morning, officer. Can I help you?'

'Officer? Do you know me? Have we met before?'

'No, but I can tell you're a policeman.'

'Oh. Well, you're right. I am. Plain clothes.'

Mrs Pargeter smiled sweetly. 'I pieced that together too. From your lack of uniform.'

'Right.' Wilkinson reached for his inside

pocket. 'Would you like to see some identification?'

'I don't really think I need to. I can tell you're the genuine article.'

'Oh.' He looked a little nonplussed and withdrew his hand.

'So ... how can I help you?'

'Well, it's a matter in relation to this car, madam,' the Inspector improvised, not very convincingly. 'We've had a report of a car of this make with this registration number having been seen in the vicinity of an area where a recent crime took place and we are following that up ...'

A look of shock came into Mrs Pargeter's innocent violet-blue eyes. 'You're not suggesting that I might have been involved in something criminal, are you, Inspector?'

'No, no, I—Here, how did you know I'm an Inspector? I didn't tell you that, did I?'

'No, you didn't, but it's self-evident.'

'Ah.' He looked puzzled, and maybe even a little flattered. 'Is it?'

'Yes. Now what is it you're suspecting me of?'

'Nothing, madam. No, we're not suspecting you of anything. It's just, as I say, the car was seen in a certain vicinity, where a certain event took place, and we are checking to see if anything was witnessed by the owner of this vehicle.'

'Ah, well ...' Mrs Pargeter smiled again. 'You don't want to be talking to me then. I'm not the owner of this vehicle.'

'You're not?'

'No, no, this is a hire car. It's owned by Gary.'

'Gary?'

She pointed. 'The chauffeur. The one who's driving.'

'Ah, right.'

'Well, not driving at the moment, but sitting in the driver's seat.'

'I see.' Wilkinson drew back. 'Sorry to have troubled you, madam.'

'No trouble at all, Inspector.' Mrs Pargeter favoured him with the beam of her biggest smile yet. 'I think the Metropolitan Police are a fine body of men, and if there's anything I can ever do to help them, I can assure you I'll do it.'

'Thank you very much, madam. I wish more members of the public shared that admirable attitude.'

Wilkinson gave Mrs Pargeter a surprisingly long look, then nodded, and she closed the window. The Inspector moved forward and was about to tap on Gary's window when he noticed it was already down.

'Anything I can do to help you, Inspector?'

'Yes, I gather you are the owner of this vehicle?'

'That is correct, yes.'

'Well, it was seen in the vicinity of an area where a recent crime took place and—'

'Which area?'

'Sorry?'

'In the vicinity of which area was my car seen?'

'Ah. Right. It was ... er ...' Wilkinson had another go at improvisation, 'round Tulse Hill.'

'And when was this?'

'Tuesday.'

'What time of day?'

'About 3 a.m.'

'Sorry, no. I haven't been to Tulse Hill since ... ooh, I don't know. Certainly not for the last year.'

'Ah, right. Well, thank you for your help. And at least I have established to whom this vehicle belongs.'

'I thought,' Mrs Pargeter's cool voice floated in from the back, 'the police had a computer system to check vehicle ownership.'

'Well, yes, we do,' said the Inspector, confused. In fact, if he'd read the printout Sergeant Hughes had given him, he would have known that the car was registered to Gary. But the obvious was never Wilkinson's way. 'On the other hand, er,' he went on, 'it sometimes pays to double-check.'

'Why?'

He tapped his nose shrewdly. 'Computers are not infallible, you know.'

'So are you saying that sometimes the old traditional methods are best?'

'Exactly, madam. How very perceptive of you to realize that.' The Inspector by now had his head halfway through Gary's window so that she could get the full benefit of his smile. There was a silence.

Eventually Mrs Pargeter broke it. 'Was there anything else we can do for you, Inspector?'

He seemed miles away. 'What? Er, no. Nothing of importance. Thank you, I have all the information I require.'

'Good.'

He continued to grin, with his head half inside the car, then suddenly recovered himself. 'Better be on my way.'

'So should we. Shouldn't we, Gary?'

'Certainly should.'

'But, er ...' Wilkinson became once again policeman-like and looked sourly down at Gary. 'Next time watch parking on the double yellow lines, eh?'

'Yes, of course, Inspector.'

'Won't do anything about it this time, but don't let me catch you doing it again—right?'

'Right.'

Still the Inspector didn't move from the side of the car. 'I think if that really is it,' said Mrs Pargeter, 'perhaps we'd better be moving on.'

'Yes. Yes, of course.' Wilkinson stood back. Gary closed his window and eased the limousine away down the road. The Inspector's eyes followed it pensively into the distance.

'What do you reckon all that was about?' Gary asked Mrs Pargeter once they were under way.

'Goodness knows.' She chuckled easily. 'Nothing to worry about, though.'

'No,' said Gary. 'No.' Then, after a

moment he added, not quite reassured, 'Why not?'

'Because,' Mrs Pargeter replied patiently, 'neither of us has done anything wrong, have we?'

'No. No, that's true.'

'So ... was it useful?' asked Sergeant Hughes eagerly when his superior was back in the surveillance car.

'Oh, yes.' The Inspector slowly stroked his chin. 'Oh, yes. It was very useful indeed.'

'In what way?'

'I'm afraid I can't be too specific on that point. Suffice it to say that there are certain moments, certain encounters in one's life which one instantly recognizes to be of enormous significance ...'

'... if one's a good copper ...?' Sergeant Hughes suggested rather sourly.

'If one is a good copper, yes. And I've a feeling that that woman I have just met will prove to be extremely significant.'

'In the case that we're working on?'

'Well, I think I can confidently state ...' But the dreamy look in the Inspector's eye was replaced by his more customary caution. 'Maybe it's better I don't answer that question for the time being.' The Sergeant's inward groan of annoyance was very nearly audible. 'No, Hughes, you just take my word for it—a good copper can recognize when someone is going to be a significant factor in ... er, any kind of operation.'

'Yes,' responded Sergeant Hughes, once again resigned to the role of dumb sidekick. 'By the way, sir, what was the lady's name?'

A shadow crossed the Inspector's craggy face. 'Do you know, I forgot to ask.'

Chapter Five

The following morning Gary's limousine eased so effortlessly along the Bayswater Road that his passengers were unaware of the constant stopping and starting necessitated by the heavy traffic. As he drove, the chauffeur gave his view of the Chastaigne Varleigh job. 'Seems to me, Mrs Pargeter, that we're going to rather a lot of unnecessary trouble. After Mrs Chastaigne snuffs it, all you need is for someone to call the police and all the paintings'll get back to their rightful owners anyway.'

Mrs Pargeter nodded. 'I know, Gary. That's what her son Toby's proposing to do. But Veronica Chastaigne doesn't want her husband's memory besmirched after she's gone.'

'Oh, right, got you.' He finessed the limousine down Kensington Church Street. 'So getting them back before she dies becomes like ...'

'Like a point of honour, yes.'

'Don't worry.' Truffler Mason gave a lugubrious grin. 'We'll soon get it sorted, Mrs P. Palings Price got the best fine art knowledge in the business.' He gestured to a narrow shopfront. 'This is it, Gary.'

The trendily minimalist graphics over the door read: 'DENZIL PRICE IN-TERIORS'. The display window was boxed in with severe grey screens. In the centre of the space, illuminated by a hidden pinpoint spotlight, stood one grey steel chair whose sharp-angled design offered all the comfort of a kebab skewer.

Gary had parked on the double yellow lines with the limousine's back door exactly opposite the shop's door, and he leapt out to usher Mrs Pargeter across the pavement.

She looked up at the name of the shop and murmured, 'If it says "Denzil", why's he called "Palings" Price?'

'Well, obvious,' said Truffler. ''Cause he used to be a fence.'

'Ah.'

The interior of the shop was as starkly minimalist as the window might have led one to expect. The grey theme was continued on the walls, floor and ceiling. The only items of furniture the room boasted were three more of the steel chairs and an angular table, clearly by the same designer. All of them showed the priority of artistic originality over comfort and function, and gave Mrs Pargeter the sensation of being in a compound surrounded by barbed wire.

Palings Price wore a voluminous suit which exactly matched the colour of the walls, and a string tie which picked out the steely gleam of the furniture. As he welcomed Truffler and Mrs Pargeter into the shop, he could not totally control a wince at the bright silk print of her dress. It threatened the uniform drabness he had worked so hard to achieve.

He gestured around the room and said, in the kind of aesthetic voice that must have got him punched a good few times at school (assuming of course that he actually had had the voice at school and not just developed it in later life), 'This, as you see, is the current Denzil Price look.'

'Ah.' Mrs Pargeter looked dutifully round, then turned back to the interior designer. 'Why?'

Palings Price was totally thrown by the question. 'What do you mean—why?'

'Why would anyone want to live in a room like this?'

'Because,' he asserted with an edge of affront, 'there are some people around who appreciate style.' He gestured to the chairs. 'Please sit down.'

Mrs Pargeter eyed the steel protrusions warily. Though she carried a lot of natural upholstery with her, she still liked a chair to make some contribution of its own. She perched on the griddle that formed the seat, and winced. 'Ooh, these people who appreciate style don't appreciate comfort, do they?'

'I can assure you, Mrs Pargeter,' said Palings Price, 'that a lot of people pay me a lot of money to make their houses look like this.'

'What sort of people?'

The interior designer smiled smugly. 'People who have everything.'

'If they've got everything—' Mrs Pargeter took in the vacancy around her, 'where on earth do they put it?'

'Elsewhere.'

'Elsewhere?'

'Yes.' He waved his hands airily around the room. 'This is not a space for putting things in—it's a space for *being* in.'

'Oh.' Mrs Pargeter's practicality asserted itself. 'So where do *you* put things?'

Palings Price hesitated for a moment, unwilling to destroy his illusion, then gave in and opened a grey door that led to the back of the shop. 'Through here.'

Mrs Pargeter looked with satisfaction at the gloryhole revealed behind the door. There was a clutter of office equipment, old chairs and piled-up files. It lacked the levels of dust, but otherwise owed more to the Truffler Mason than the Denzil Price school of interior design.

'Ah. That looks more comfy,' said Mrs Pargeter, and immediately moved through to park her dented rump into the soft recesses of a broken-down armchair.

A few minutes later, Truffler was also ensconced in a comfortable chair in the back room. Only Palings Price looked ill at ease on upholstery. Maybe his bottom was of such high aesthetic sensibility that it could only appreciate furniture which made a design statement.

His eyes narrowed as he took in the typewritten list that Truffler had just handed him. He seemed surprised by its contents. 'Well, I can tell you where most of these came from straight off. One or two'll take a bit of research, though.'

'We'd be very glad if you'd undertake that research for us, Palings.'

The interior designer couldn't quite hide the wince that Truffler's use of his nickname induced, but he quickly covered it with a bonhomous smile. 'Of course. Anything for the widow of the late Mr Pargeter.' She smiled her customary acknowledgement of this recurrent compliment. Palings Price looked across at the private investigator. 'You want a list of premises robbed and dates when the goods were lifted—that right, Truffler?'

'Right.'

The list seemed to exert a mesmeric fascination. Palings Price looked at it again, shook his head and let out a low whistle. 'It's good stuff, this. Some of the most famous art thefts of the last twenty years.'

'Yes.'

'And all together in the one collection at the moment, is it?' Truffler Mason nodded. 'Could I hazard a guess at the collector's name ...?' Palings Price went on. 'Lou Ronson ...? Sultan of Arbat ...? Sticky Fingers Frampton ...?'

But Truffler wasn't rising to the bait. 'I think this is one occasion, Palings, when the less detail you know the better.'

'Funny,' Mrs Pargeter observed innocently. 'That's what my husband always used to say to me, Truffler.'

Chapter Six

'How did Palings Price get all his knowledge of fine art?' asked Mrs Pargeter, as the limousine sped silkily on its return journey.

'Oh, he done all the legit training,' Truffler replied. 'University. Galleries. Then worked for one of the big auction houses. Left there under something of a cloud, I'm afraid.'

'Ah.'

'Trouble is, places like that, they tend to count the Goyas at the end of the day.'

'Yes, yes, I suppose they would.'

'Nothing they could pin on him, of course, but, er ... well, mud does tend to stick, doesn't it?'

'So I've heard.'

'Anyway, he never looked back, career-wise. I mean, he helped your husband in, like, an advisory capacity, but lots of other people used him too. He never worked exclusively for Mr P. Oh no, his services was very much in demand.'

Mrs Pargeter thought she probably shouldn't enquire which particular services these were, and fortunately Truffler needed no prompting to spell it out. 'Paling's speciality used to be *very* private collections.'

'How do you mean?'

'There's still a lot of millionaires out there desperate to own something unique.'

'Like a world-famous painting, say ...?'

'You got it.'

'... that they can gloat over on their own in a gallery nobody else is allowed to enter ...?'

Truffler nodded. 'Palings used to procure the paintings and design the galleries where they was to be hung.'

'Do you reckon he still does that kind of stuff?'

'Shouldn't think so.' The detective let out a mournful chuckle. 'If he can get well-heeled boneheads to pay him for painting their rooms grey, taking all the furniture out and making them sit on cheese-graters, why bother?'

Mrs Pargeter grinned agreement. The limousine had come to a rest in front of the distinguished façade of Greene's Hotel.

'Thanks, Gary,' she said as the chauffeur ushered her out. 'You'd better be off to fetch that MP from Heathrow.'

'Right. Give us a call if you need me.'

'Sure. Cheerio.' And as Gary got back into the car, she called after him, 'And don't forget to send me an invoice!'

He grinned. This was part of a running battle between them. Gary, out of gratitude for all that the late Mr Pargeter had done

49

for his career, was keen to provide the man's widow with free chauffeuring. Mrs Pargeter, who knew how difficult it could be to start up a new business, was adamant about paying at the proper rate.

As the limousine slipped away, she looked up with some satisfaction at her current home.

The elegance of Greene's Hotel, ravishingly set in one of London's most exclusive squares, was so understated it almost hurt. The hotel provided an environment in which every whim was anticipated. No sooner had the shadow of a desire for something crossed the brain of a guest than a member of staff had glided into place with the required object neatly presented on a silver salver. The atmosphere of Greene's was so rarefied that its guests were never allowed to think about things as mundane as money (which is just as well, considering how much their stay there is costing them).

The irony that this temple to gracious living should be run by a gentleman known in a former existence as 'Hedgeclipper' Clinton was never lost on Mrs Pargeter. He was another name from the address book of the late Mr Pargeter, and had worked for her husband in rather less elegant surroundings than Greene's Hotel. The precise nature of the services he had provided was unclear, though a clue to his methods of persuasion and enforcement could be found—by those who were interested in such matters—in his nickname. Mrs Pargeter herself was not interested. During her long and happy marriage to the late Mr Pargeter, she had quickly learnt that there were many subjects related to her husband's business affairs in which there was no point in her taking any interest at all.

Mrs Pargeter was now a semi-permanent resident of Greene's Hotel. She had tried other forms of accommodation, but found them wanting. She was in theory having a dream house built in which to pass her 'declining years', but the builder, who delighted in the nickname of 'Concrete' Jacket, had proved—through no fault of his own—frequently absent from the project. As a result, progress on the construction was slow, and in the interim Mrs Pargeter contented herself with the surroundings of a luxury hotel.

The shadow of desire cast across her brain that evening as she entered the hotel with Truffler Mason was for champagne. As ever, her whim was anticipated by the barman Leon (not, in this instance, a particularly difficult feat of mind-reading—Mrs Pargeter almost always felt like champagne in the early evening). Immediately the bottle was open and on ice. Two crystal glasses stood in readiness on her favourite table in the room which looked more like the library of a country house than anything so common as a bar.

Demonstrating the sense of priorities which she had maintained throughout her life, Mrs Pargeter saw the two glasses filled by Leon, Truffler toasted, and substantial swallows taken, before she moved back to business. 'Palings seemed pretty certain that some of the paintings were from galleries abroad. Does that raise any problems, Truffler?'

'Shouldn't do.'

'Oh. You mean you know how to smuggle fine art out of the country?'

He gave an arch grin. 'No, I don't know how to do it myself. But I know a man who does.'

Mrs Pargeter smiled and took another tingling swallow of champagne. It was

52

wonderful, she reflected, how things interconnected. Her late husband's network had been *so* well-organized. Whatever expertise was required, someone in the system would always know of the right person to call on. And they always obliged so readily. Though she regretted no longer having the husband himself, she did have the next best thing. Not a day went by without her feeling the care and love with which the late Mr Pargeter continued to look after her from beyond the grave.

'Actually,' Truffler's voice broke into her reverie, 'you know the man I'm talking about.'

'Do I? Who is it?'

The detective grinned. 'HRH.'

'Oh, goodie,' said Mrs Pargeter. 'Now he's someone I'd really like to see again.'

Chapter Seven

The flat in which Detective Inspector Craig Wilkinson spent as little time as possible was only one step up from a bedsitter, and demonstrated as many little personal touches as the average policeman's office. Indeed, the flat's sitting room was virtually identical to the office where the Inspector worked at the station. It had the same cream walls and 1950s metal window frames. The curtains were institutional green and, on the rare occasions they were pulled across, gave an uneven striped effect from years of bunched bleaching by the sun. Furniture was minimal and functional—chairs with scuffed light wood arms and prolapsed seats in green mock leather, a table whose Formica top was scarred and pitted with old cigarette burns. Though the kitchen was rarely used for cooking, just as a depository for the foil and polystyrene boxes of takeaways, it still contrived to be extremely grimy. When he walked in there the Inspector's soles made a slight sucking sound against the sticky linoleum.

And the atmosphere of the flat was heavy with the smell of long-dead cigarettes.

Still, Craig Wilkinson had years before ceased to be aware of his surroundings, and it was a long time since anyone else had been there to notice them. Nowadays he had the same attitude to sex as he did to promotion. Since all attempts were doomed to failure, it was hardly worth filling in the metaphorical application forms. What was the point of going through the elaborate—and expensive—rigmarole of chatting up, buying drinks for, buying meals for, and luring back home, someone with whom it was never going to work out from the start? Wilkinson found that, as he progressed through his fifties, his libido had shrunk till it was like some residual nub of an organ left behind by the evolutionary process, a vermiform appendix whose function wasn't quite clear. The Inspector did sometimes still have romantic thoughts, but he very rarely had erotic ones.

The predominant thoughts he had when he was in the flat tended to be gloomy ones, which was why he spent the minimum amount of time possible there. Sitting alone, puffing on another cigarette, he would become obsessed by old fiascos and frustrations, by the failures in both his private and professional lives. Because, in spite of what he had hinted at to Sergeant Hughes, Inspector Wilkinson had never really 'made his mark' in the Police Force. Nor, it has to be said, had he 'made his mark' significantly at an emotional level. The attitude of his former wife to him was one of undiluted contempt and, so far as he could tell, none of his other women remembered him as anything other than a mildly distasteful detour from the main ongoing journey of their lives.

But, in spite of all this, Craig Wilkinson was not a pessimist. Gloomy and grumpy he might be, but it never occurred to him for a moment that his aspirations were at an end, that he was destined never to 'make his mark'. Oh no, in his heart of hearts, he knew it would still happen. He'd left it late perhaps, but he, Detective Inspector Craig Wilkinson, was still going to be remembered as a remarkable detective.

He had long since recognized that his basic problem was one of identity. The worlds of television cop shows, which he watched avidly, and crime fiction, which he read avidly, were full of truly individual policemen, quirky, gifted, eccentric, bolshie, hard-drinking, unlikely, but, above all, memorable. There were even one or two such men and women—though obviously many less—in the world of the real Police Force. And Inspector Wilkinson longed passionately to join their number.

The trouble was that police work

remained an incredibly painstaking and repetitive business. It was, not to put too fine a point on it, as boring as hell. And this quality was one which the Inspector's character, in spite of any wishes he might have for himself, reflected all too accurately.

At times he'd tried to make himself more interesting by grafting characteristics on to his personality. There had been experiments with alcohol. Booze, after all, was the natural accompaniment to the long lonely sessions of self-recrimination in his flat. He should be one of those cops who was never without a bottle at the bedside, a hip flask in the raincoat pocket. Every morning he should wake up with a brain-crushing hangover, but still somehow manage the day's work. He should get into fights and smash up furniture in bars. It would be entirely appropriate—indeed the perfect solution to his lack of identity—for Craig Wilkinson to be a cop with a drink problem.

The trouble was, he didn't like the taste of alcohol that much. He wasn't teetotal, but found that after a couple of drinks he'd had enough and didn't want any more. What he really enjoyed was sitting down with a nice cup of tea, a cigarette, and a packet of chocolate bourbon biscuits.

He also disliked the way alcohol affected his stomach. Even more, he disliked the way it affected his judgement. Craig Wilkinson hated to feel that he was losing control at any level.

So, whatever his route to becoming a memorable cop was, it wouldn't be as a boozer.

Still, there are other ways, he thought to himself the evening after he'd met the woman in the limousine, other ways I can 'make my mark'. I'm not finished yet, by any manner of means.

He sat in his institutional green armchair, lighted cigarette in hand, with a pot of tea and an open packet of chocolate bourbon biscuits, and for once his mind wasn't flooded with gloom. The old thoughts of past failures were there, sure enough, but they didn't swamp him. Now he had a glimmer of hope. Now there was something he could achieve, something so magnificent that it would pay off all debts, eclipse all memories of the operations that had not worked out for him.

Yes, even of the big one, the one whose recollection never failed to bring him a new pang of disappointment. He had been so close then, so very close. As usual, he had taken the 'softly, softly catchee monkey' approach. He had started with a tip-off from an informer, an anonymous voice at the end of a telephone line who called himself 'Posey Narker'. That initial contact had been expensive, but worth every penny.

And from that first detail Wilkinson had built up a huge database of information. He had resisted the temptation to rush, to pick up minor villains as soon as he had enough evidence to convict them. He had waited, patiently watching link join to link, seeing where the operations of one villain overlapped with those of another, until he had almost mapped out the complete network.

And he had watched, with mounting excitement, the direction in which these lines of connection pointed. He had seen how they were all converging, all coming together till they met in one man, the spider at the centre of the huge complex web.

And Wilkinson had identified that man, built up a dossier of evidence against him. He'd been within an ace of catching the man, of putting him under arrest and sending out wider and wider ripples of lesser arrests until the whole organization would have been under lock and key.

Would have been. Would have been ... if something hadn't gone wrong.

But something had gone wrong. And it had left Inspector Wilkinson seething with frustration for the rest of his life.

Until now. Now he had a glimmer of a hope of a possibility of staging something that would settle the old scores for good. Once this was sorted, no one would ever forget the name of Detective Inspector Craig Wilkinson.

He poured himself some more tea, puffed on his cigarette, and picked up a fresh chocolate bourbon biscuit. Once this was sorted, he reflected, everything he did would become trendsetting. The role model for all future detectives would be of a tough, hardbitten tea-drinker who liked chocolate bourbon biscuits.

As he thought this heart-warming thought, Craig Wilkinson mouthed silently, confidently to himself, the name of his old adversary. 'Oh yes, I think I'm about to erase all memories of the failure I had in nailing you down ... Mr Pargeter.'

Chapter Eight

The Indian summer was continuing. It was a glowing, golden September morning. An unobtrusive brass plate on the portico of the splendid Berkeley Square frontage identified the offices of 'HRH Travel'. Mrs Pargeter billowed elegantly through the front door and was greeted by a perfectly uniformed girl, whose gold name-badge revealed that she was called 'Lauren', and who had risen from her Reception desk as if forewarned of the new arrival.

'Mrs Pargeter, isn't it?' she enunciated beautifully, making a statement rather than a question, and proffering an immaculately manicured hand.

Mrs Pargeter shook the hand and readily acknowledged her identity. 'You've got a good memory, Lauren. Been a while since I've been in here.'

'HRH is very keen that we should always remember our clients' names. Particularly our most important clients.' Mrs Pargeter knew this was only professional flannel, but still found it comforting. 'HRH is expecting you,' the girl continued, as she pressed a button on her desk and announced, 'Sharon, Mrs Pargeter is here.'

In a matter of moments Sharon appeared. Like Lauren, she was fastidiously well-groomed and dressed in the same expensively cut charcoal-grey uniform with a small 'HRH' logo worked in gold thread on the breast pocket. 'Mrs Pargeter, how very good to see you again,' Sharon elocuted enthusiastically. 'If you'd like to follow me to the lift, HRH is really looking forward to seeing you.'

On the first floor Mrs Pargeter was escorted along the aisle of a high-tech open-plan office. On either side more immaculate girls in charcoal-grey uniforms sat at computers or talked on telephones. As she passed, Mrs Pargeter heard fragments of their conversations.

'... that our representative will meet you at the Lagos Hilton with all the documentation in your new name. Just look out for the HRH logo ...'

'... but at Athens airport make sure you put the bag with the gun in through the *right-hand* x-ray machine. That will be malfunctioning at the time ...'

'... to let you know that your tickets will arrive by courier this afternoon, along with tourist guidebooks, a plan of the bank interior and exterior, and a map showing the route the bullion van will be taking ...'

'... you'll have no problem fitting the body into the windsurfer carrying-case. It could have been designed for the purpose ...'

'... Good heavens, no! The Passport Control officers will already have *been* bribed. It's all part of the HRH service ...'

Mrs Pargeter was, as ever, reassured by the efficiency and attention to detail that characterized HRH Travel.

The company's founder stood in the doorway of his office to greet her. Tall, distinguished, olive-skinned, with almost operatic white hair and moustache, Hamish Ramon Henriques was dressed in another of his punctiliously cut tweed three-piece suits. That, coupled with the regimental tie, gave off an aura of old money, reliability and a world in which no guarantees were required other than the handshake of a gentleman.

The handshake of a gentleman that

he gave to Mrs Pargeter was warm and enthusiastic. He beamed, his black eyes sparkled, as he welcomed her in his old-school tones. 'Such a pleasure, Mrs Pargeter. Been far too long. Such an unqualified delight to see you. Such a pleasure.'

They sat in his office over the tray with silver coffee pot and bone china cups that had been brought in by a charcoal-grey-suited girl called Karen, and Mrs Pargeter politely asked Hamish Ramon Henriques about the progress of his business.

'Can't complain, can't complain,' he replied. 'Everything absolutely tickety-boo, in fact. And improving all the time, I'm glad to say. Most businesses are becoming global these days. As a result, everyone's travelling more—which can only be good news for an organization like mine.'

'And is it the same sort of destinations it's always been?'

'Well, those continue to be popular— Costa del Sol, South America ... Changes a bit according to which countries make extradition treaties, of course, but it's steady business. Also doing a lot of work now with what used to be called the Eastern Bloc. That's opening up a lot.

Then Malaysia, Indonesia, Thailand, you know ... Even starting to do quite a bit in China.' Hamish Ramon Henriques smiled a complacent smile. 'One of the unfailing rules of economics, you know—wherever capitalism goes, criminals will quickly follow. And if there's one thing criminals are always going to need, it's transport.'

An unfocused mistiness had come into Mrs Pargeter's eyes. The look frequently appeared there when 'criminals' were mentioned. It was almost as if she had an allergy to the word. 'Well,' she said vaguely, 'I wouldn't know about that.'

HRH seemed to realize he had transgressed some invisible barrier between them. 'No, of course not,' he agreed hastily. 'And no reason why you ever should.' Moving the conversation on to safer ground, he asked, 'Anyway, what can I do for you this bright and beautiful morning, Mrs Pargeter?'

'Well,' she began tentatively, 'I hope it's not too much trouble ...'

'A contradiction in terms! Positive oxymoron—the idea that anything I might undertake for you could be too much trouble. I and my entire staff are at your disposal for whatever you should require.

Oh, Mrs Pargeter, when I think back to how much your husband did for me in the early days of my career—'

'Yes, yes.' It wasn't that she didn't appreciate this litany of thanks to the late Mr Pargeter; it was just that she had heard it so many times before. 'What I need, HRH, is help in the transportation of some paintings.'

'And would these be paintings whose ...' he paused, selecting his words with punctilious discretion 'whose provenance might be such that their transportation should not be ... too public ...?'

'Exactly.' Mrs Pargeter appreciated his quick understanding of her problem.

'And may I ask which countries will be involved in the transportation of the paintings?'

'Quite a few. Certainly France, Germany and Spain. I think there might even be some that have to go back to the States. Maybe even Japan. Will that be a problem?'

'Good heavens, no,' Hamish Ramon Henriques replied breezily. 'Compared to other jobs I have undertaken ... compared to Lord Lucan ... compared to Shergar—never easy when you're dealing with horseboxes ... No, a few paintings will be nothing—whichever countries happen to be involved.' He paused. 'One thing you said, Mrs Pargeter ...'

'Yes?'

'I didn't mishear you saying that these paintings needed to "go back"?'

'Yes. They all need to go back to where they were—' she corrected herself seamlessly, 'to where they started from.'

'Fine.'

HRH did not ask for further explanation, but Mrs Pargeter supplied it nonetheless. 'You see, someone's asked me to arrange it, and I've said I would. And with me ... well, when I say I'm going to do something, it's kind of a point of honour that I see it actually gets done.'

'I understand completely, Mrs Pargeter. It would be exactly the same in my own case.' He emitted a fruity little chuckle. 'Where would one be in business if one could not trust the good faith and the word of a gentleman?'

'My feeling entirely, HRH. So, going back to the paintings ... have you done that kind of thing before?'

'I have been involved in many comparable operations, yes. There is a very simple standard procedure to follow.' He gave a thoughtful twirl to his moustache. 'It does, however, involve the cooperation of one other person ...'

'Who's that?'

'Have you heard of someone called "VVO"?'

Mrs Pargeter shook her head and observed, 'Lot of initials in this business, aren't there, HRH?'

Chapter Nine

The unmarked car was parked at the same beauty spot overlooking Chastaigne Varleigh. So far the only arrival and departure noted down on Sergeant Hughes's clipboard was that of the milkman.

As well as smoke, the car was full of the sound of Wagner. Trying another initiative in his continuing search for individual identity as a detective, Inspector Wilkinson had invested in the complete *Ring* cycle on cassette. Deciding not to prejudice the experience by reading the notes or synopsis, he had started at the beginning with *Rheingold.* It has to be said he didn't find it very accessible. Of course he wasn't aware that he was listening to the dwarf Alberich's encounter with the river maidens, Woglinde, Wellgunde and Flosshilde, but it probably wouldn't have made much difference if he had been. Craig Wilkinson was not very musical.

Sergeant Hughes was, but his tastes ran more to grunge and funk than Wagner.

They survived over an hour of the *Ring* cycle without either of them making any comment. Then the Inspector reached forward and switched off the cassette player. 'I think I kind of get the feeling of that,' he lied. 'But better not listen to too much at one go. Give myself a bit of time to assimilate what I've already heard. Wouldn't you agree?'

'Yes,' said the Sergeant, investing the monosyllable with more enthusiasm than usual.

There was a long silence. Down at Chastaigne Varleigh nothing was happening. Maybe somewhere in the world something was happening, but it seemed to Sergeant Hughes a very long time since anything had happened to him. He was beginning to feel as if his entire life had been spent in that car with Inspector Wilkinson.

'I think the moment has come, Hughes,' said the Inspector, breaking the silence, 'when I should tell you something.'

'Like what?'

'Something related to the case on which we are working.'

Not before bloody time, thought Sergeant Hughes. But he didn't say it. Though his exasperation had been mounting with every minute they spent together, he still recognized that certain professional courtesies had to be observed. He waited, allowing Wilkinson to make his revelations at his own pace.

Being Wilkinson, that pace was a pretty slow one. 'For some years now, Hughes,' the Inspector began, 'I have been trying to make connections between a series of crimes. They're all art thefts. I have been going through the files in considerable detail, checking similarities of method, finding other parallels and comparisons. I've read through extensive witness statements, and conducted follow-up interviews. I have collated masses of data, and am very close to identifying the common thread which links all the individual crimes.'

He was silent. Sergeant Hughes waited an appropriate length of time, but since nothing else was apparently forthcoming, asked, 'And is this common thread a person?'

'It is, yes.'

'A criminal mastermind?'

The Inspector winced. 'I don't like the use of that expression. It engenders defeatism. A mastermind is, by definition, someone of superior intellect, but no criminal has an intellect which is *that* superior. There is no criminal so clever that he cannot be caught out by the painstaking, methodical police work of a good copper.'

Sergeant Hughes was not convinced of this assertion—at least in relation to Inspector Wilkinson. If it was him, Hughes, conducting the case, things'd be different. He had flair, intuition, skill, subtlety—all the qualities his boss so patently lacked. Still, it wasn't the moment to argue. The Inspector was finally giving him some facts about the case they were working on, and it would be foolish to divert him. So all the Sergeant said was, 'Right, sir.'

'Oh yes ...' Wilkinson nodded slowly.

71

'Oh yes, all the information seems to lead back to one name.'

'And do you reckon you've got enough solid evidence to arrest him?'

'Well ...' The Inspector grimaced. 'Well, I might have, but there are certain logistical problems inherent in the idea of arresting this particular individual.'

'What kind of logistical problems?'

'Well, the main one is—he's dead.'

'Ah. Ah, yes. Well, I can see that might slow you down a bit, sir.'

'However, in the case of theft, the death of the perpetrator does not necessarily close the case.'

'No. The case is still open until the stolen property has been recovered and returned to its rightful owner.'

Inspector Wilkinson looked slightly miffed at having his narrative hurried along in this way. He gave his junior a sour look. 'Yes, Hughes. Precisely.'

'And you reckon, in this instance, the stolen property is in Chastaigne Varleigh?'

But this was going unacceptably fast. However far his own conjectures might have progressed in that direction, Wilkinson certainly wasn't yet ready to share them with an underling. 'No, Hughes,' he said. 'I am still investigating their precise whereabouts.'

'But if they're not in Chastaigne Varleigh, then why are we spending all this time watching the place?'

'I have my reasons,' the Inspector replied loftily. 'Remember, Hughes, you are the junior member of this team. I am the strategist. I work out what we do, why we do it, and when we do it. The case we are involved in here is one of enormous complexity, which will not respond well to being rushed. I will decide when the moment is right for all the individual threads of the case to be pulled together. And that moment is certainly not yet.' A finger rose to his nose for the trademark tap. 'One of the secrets of being a good copper, Hughes, is to have an infallible instinct for timing.'

'Yes,' the Sergeant agreed flatly. Then, after a moment's silence, he ventured, 'You did say you were going to tell me something related to the case we're working on.'

The Inspector was affronted. 'I *have* told you something.'

'Not much.'

'I've told you the case involves a series

of art thefts. And I've told you that all of these art thefts seem to lead back to one man.'

'One dead man.'

'Exactly.' Wilkinson was appalled that the Sergeant wasn't more appreciative of the generosity with which this information had been shared. 'What more do you want to know?'

'The man's name perhaps ...?'

The Inspector shook his head, very slowly. 'Need to know, Hughes, need to know. Why do you *need to know* that information?'

'Well, it might help me help you with the investigation, mightn't it?'

This prompted another, even slower, shake of the head. 'We have no proof it would do that.'

'But, for heaven's sake ...!' Sergeant Hughes burst out in exasperation. A look at the Inspector's expression, however, deterred him from pressing further. He sank back grumpily into his seat. There was a very long silence.

The last exchange had triggered a decision in the Sergeant's mind. The frustration engendered by working with Inspector Wilkinson had been building all the time, and Hughes had been increasingly tempted to begin investigating on his own. Their most recent exchange had made his mind up. The files of Wilkinson's previous researches were bound still to be around the station. It would be easy to dig out the relevant ones and go through them.

Sergeant Hughes was sure that a mind of his quality would very quickly overtake whatever progress his dinosaur of a boss might have achieved. Hughes visualized the satisfaction of sewing the whole case up on his own, the accolades he would receive, the recommendations for promotion—above all, the expression that would appear on Wilkinson's face when he saw that he'd finally been relegated to the rank of yesterday's man. Oh yes, thought the Sergeant, I am bloody well going to crack this case—on my own.

His boss's voice invaded these gleeful fantasies. 'Try a bit more of the Wagner, shall we?'

Hughes met this suggestion with an almost inaudible grunt.

'No, perhaps not,' Inspector Wilkinson decided.

Chapter Ten

The room looked like the first attempt of a tyro set designer to produce the studio of a tortured artist. There was a bit too much of everything—too much paint spilled on the floor, too many dirty buckets, battered paint pots, spattered palettes, cracking easels and paint-hardened rags. The room seemed to boom out in over-elaborate shorthand: I reflect the image of a nonconforming bohemian.

The actual artwork on display amidst the cluttered chaos confused the image even further, prompting the suspicion that perhaps this was not the studio of one individual artist, but of a collection of artists, all working in different styles. Every school of painting from the old masters onwards seemed to be represented. *Pietàs* and altarpieces rubbed shoulders with blurred impressionists; Russian icons faced up to pop art swirls; titled ladies in eighteenth-century frocks stared dubiously at twentieth-century abstracts. All the paintings looked to be genuine representatives of their schools; the only detail that cast doubt on their validity was that most of them were unfinished.

The artist whose personality these conflicting images presumably reflected also looked a bit overdone. One might have accepted the wild matted hair, the beret, *or* the filthy smock; the presence of all three seemed a bit over the top. His manic-depressive manner, in which moods of gloom alternated suddenly with wild bursts of elation, was also a little too studied. As he sat at a paint-spattered table, a half-empty bottle of red wine clutched in his desperate hand, he seemed an assemblage of artistic clichés rather than someone whose eccentricity was a spontaneous expression of personality.

He looked across at his guests with malevolent despair. Mrs Pargeter and HRH perched gingerly on dilapidated armchairs. Though she had shown no qualms about sitting on the dust in Truffler Mason's office, Mrs Pargeter looked less certain of the hygienic standards of this place. She had no wish to add further smudges of colour to the vibrant pattern of her fine silk dress.

'So ... I'm "VVO". Welcome to my humble studio.' The artist flung out a despondent gesture which encompassed the whole room, and slopped more of his wine bottle's contents into a chipped enamel mug.

'Thank you,' said Mrs Pargeter politely. 'One thing HRH wouldn't tell me ... he said I should ask you myself ... is what "VVO" stands for ...?'

Hamish Ramon Henriques smiled quietly, as the artist shrugged another gesture of despair. 'Huh,' he grunted bitterly. 'It's a joke that was made at my expense by some of ... some of the people HRH and I work with from time to time.'

'Yes?' Mrs Pargeter prompted.

The bitterness grew deeper, as VVO went on, 'just because I take my art seriously ... just because it matters to me ... they nicknamed me after one of the great geniuses of my profession—Vincent Van Gogh.'

'I see.' Mrs Pargeter was silent for a moment before asking the inevitable question. 'Then why aren't you called "VVG"?'

'I told you. They made a mockery of me.' The misunderstood one took another angry slurp from his mug, as he spelled out the detail of his humiliation. 'They called me "Vincent Vin Ordinaire".'

Hamish Ramon Henriques ran a hand through the luxuriance of his moustache to prevent his smile from becoming too overt, and Mrs Pargeter was glad she wasn't in eye contact with him, as she soothed the injured genius with the meaningless words, 'Oh. Oh well, that's nice.'

But VVO's well of bitterness was far from dry. 'They're always making fun of me,' he moaned on, 'laughing at my aspirations to be a great artist ... dismissing my paintings as mere imitative daubs ...'

'Oh, come on,' HRH protested. 'We always respected what you did best.'

The artist was incensed. 'No, you didn't! You respected my hack work!' Fuelled by anger, he rose from his seat and started to circle the room. 'You respected me when I produced a Rubens.'

As he spoke, he picked up a canvas of a buxom nude whose bottom blushed appealingly. Mrs Pargeter, who had seen a similar sight in the bathroom mirror earlier that morning, could not restrain herself from murmuring, 'Oh, that's very good.'

'Or a Goya,' VVO went on vindictively,

picking up a lady wearing a black mantilla whose authenticity was only let down by an unpainted patch of canvas in the top corner.

Though this picture struck no personal chords, Mrs Pargeter could still recognize the skill of its execution. 'That's smashing too,' she said.

'Or a Jackson Pollock.' On this third canvas, however, she could express no opinion. Mrs Pargeter had always found it tricky to tell a good Jackson Pollock from a bad one—or indeed from an accident in a paint shop.

The tortured genius let all three canvases clatter to the floor, as he struck his chest in impassioned misery. 'But what happens when I express *myself* ... when I do a painting that is a true *Reg Winthrop?*'

To reinforce his words, he picked up a picture which had stood facing the wall. It was fixed in a gold frame, and was quite definitely the ugliest work of art Mrs Pargeter had ever seen. No weekend painter, suffering from a terminal overdose of sentimentality, could ever have produced worse.

A black Scottie dog, with an anthropo-morphic smile and a tartan bow about its neck, sat coquettishly in front of a little humpbacked bridge over a tinkling stream. Spotted toadstools poked up through the grass. Bluebirds circled aimlessly overhead. The painting could have won a Queen's Award for Winsomeness. Even a chocolate-box manufacturer would have rejected it as too coy.

'Hmm ...' said Mrs Pargeter awkwardly. 'Well, yes ...'

'See!' VVO let the painting slip from his hand and hurled himself histrionically back into his chair. 'You're just like all the others. You can't appreciate what I'm really trying to say. You can't see through to the soul of my art. Ah, is it always the fate of genius to be misunderstood?'

Hamish Ramon Henriques decided that pursuing such speculation would be fruitless. It was time to get down to business. 'VVO, in fact the reason we are here is that—'

But the artist's list of grievances was not exhausted. 'Not only does nobody appreciate my painting, I'm also excluded from all the exciting bits when we've got a job on. I'm always left on the sidelines. While the rest of the lads are having fun, out and about breaking and entering,

I'm always stuck back here knocking out another Rembrandt.'

HRH waved an impatient hand. 'Yes, VVO, I've heard all this before. Listen, we need your help for a job.'

'Painting again, I suppose?' the artist sneered. 'No breaking and entering. No immobilizing burglar alarms. I'd be good at all that! You're wasting the talents of a criminal genius, you know!'

But HRH was impervious to these demands for sympathy. 'The job,' he confirmed, 'is, as you guessed, painting.' At these words, VVO slumped even deeper into his chair. 'Quite a lot of painting. Some old masters and some more modern works of art need to travel abroad. We want cover paintings for them.'

The artistic worm turned. 'Oh, no! Have you really got the nerve to ask me to do that kind of stuff again?'

'It is,' HRH pointed out discreetly, 'for Mrs Pargeter.' He let the words sink in before adding, 'Widow of the late Mr Pargeter.'

Her husband's name worked its customary magic. After a baleful look at HRH, the artist conceded, 'Oh, all right, I'll do your pathetic little job—even though it's a prostitution of my art.' Then he slumped back again with his eyes closed.

'Everyone has to make compromises in this life, VVO.'

All that got was a 'Huh.'

'And I'll tell you what ... the modern art covers can be anything you want ...' One of VVO's eyes flicked open. 'You could even make them Reg Winthrops, if you like ...'

Though it went against the character he had created for himself to show it at all fulsomely, this news clearly pleased the artist.

Hamish Ramon Henriques rubbed his hands together briskly. 'Anyway, you're forgetting your manners. Aren't you going to offer us a drink?'

VVO looked at his guests with renewed truculence. 'Do you want something?'

Mrs Pargeter didn't want to put her host to any trouble. 'I'm happy with some of that wine if you—'

'No, no!' As if his artistic integrity was being impugned, the painter clutched his bottle to his chest. 'The wine's mine, all mine!'

'Oh very well. A cup of tea'd be nice then.'

VVO immediately shouted to some unseen presence outside the room, 'Tea, woman! Bring us tea!' He turned grumpily to HRH. 'When will you bring me the paintings?'

'Next couple of days. There are more than thirty of them. You think you'll be able to do the covers within the week?'

After the animation of the shouted tea order, the artist had slumped back into apathy. 'What does it matter what I think?' he asked from the recesses of his chair. 'Of course I can do them. Like any true genius, I work fast.'

There was a silence. Mrs Pargeter wondered who would bring the tea. With what kind of woman would someone like VVO cohabit? Which stereotype of the artist's muse would it be? Some sluttish student with fiercely dyed hair and nose-jewellery? A former life model, blowsy and gone to seed? A hippy trailing scarves and wispy skirts?

The interior door opened to reveal none of the above. The woman who stood there with a neat tray of tea things was neatly dressed as a neat, ultra-conventional suburban housewife. The decor revealed behind her showed a neat, ultra-conventional suburban sitting room.

'Good afternoon,' said the woman politely. 'I'm Deirdre Winthrop, Reg's wife.'

She cleared a space on a cluttered table, put down the tea tray and turned with hand outstretched.

Mrs Pargeter shook it. 'Good afternoon. I'm Mrs Pargeter.'

HRH went through the same social routine. Shaking his hostess's hand, he identified himself as Hamish Ramon Henriques.

'Pleased to meet you both, I'm sure.' Deirdre Winthrop smiled graciously. 'Tea was it you said you'd like?'

'That'd be lovely, thank you,' said Mrs Pargeter, with an equally gracious smile.

Deirdre lifted the wine bottle out of her husband's unprotesting hands. 'And you want some more of your blackcurrant juice, love?'

Reg Winthrop grinned at his wife, very calmly and with great fondness. 'Yes, please, my angel,' he replied, the picture of meek suburban domesticity.

Mrs Pargeter and Hamish Ramon Henriques exchanged looks, but made no comment.

Chapter Eleven

Mrs Pargeter's customary shadow of desire had been anticipated again that evening by Leon the barman. The champagne was on ice, the two crystal glasses waited in readiness. And, standing over her favourite table as she entered the room, massaging his hands in unctuous delight, stood the proprietor of Greene's Hotel, Mr Clinton. 'Mrs Pargeter,' he oozed, as he filled one of the glasses with swelling bubbles. 'How delightful to see you. I trust you have had an enjoyable day.'

'Very pleasant, thanks. Met an artist by the name of Reg Winthrop. Do you know him, by any chance?'

'Winthrop ... Winthrop ...?' the hotel manager mused. 'No, I don't believe the name means anything to me.'

'He's also known as "VVO".'

'Ah.' His expression cleared. 'Yes, of course. Another employee of your late husband.'

'So I'm given to understand, yes.'

'And in fact someone who has worked for me in the not-too-distant past.'

'Really?'

The hotel manager smiled. 'The artwork in some of the more expensive suites—like the Gainsborough in your own, Mrs Pargeter—well, with the best will in the world, one would of course like them to be genuine ... but the fact remains that, if they were the real thing, certain of my guests—not of course you, I hasten to add—might be tempted to purloin them.'

'I'm surprised to hear people of that kind come to this hotel.'

'Oh, indeed, Mrs Pargeter, you are right. All of my clients are absolutely out of the top drawer, people of impeccable ethical standards, but—' he grimaced as he spelled out the unpalatable truth—'when it comes to art, normal moral considerations go out of the window. I'm afraid the zeal of the collector is too powerful, and the presence of genuinely valuable paintings in the suites would prove just too much of a temptation to some people. So it is simpler if I decorate the rooms with VVO's very fine copies.'

'Isn't there a danger that those copies might get stolen?'

The hotel manager looked affronted. 'Good heavens, no, Mrs Pargeter. The kind of clients who frequent Greene's Hotel would recognize instantly that they were fakes.'

Further discussion of the vagaries of the rich was prevented by the arrival of Truffler Mason, wearing his customary shapeless brown suit and his customary undertaker's frown. 'Hi there, Mrs P, Hedgeclipper,' he said joylessly.

The hotel manager winced. '*If* you don't mind ... within the purlieus of this hotel, it is preferred that nicknames are not used, Mr Mason.'

'Sorry, Mr Clinton.'

'Think nothing of it.' Hedgeclipper was once again wreathed in smiles. 'Now, if you will excuse me ... I have to arrange a fleet of stretch limos for the Sultan's wives ...' And he wafted imperceptibly out of the room.

Mrs Pargeter charged her guest's glass with champagne and raised hers to toast him. 'So, Truffler, can you fill me in a bit more on what HRH told me? When the paintings leave the country, they are actually declared to Customs?'

'Well, *some* paintings are, yes. VVO's

modern rubbish. That's what the customs inspectors see.'

'But the real ones are hidden underneath?'

'Exactly. Don't worry, it's a doddle. HRH has organized that kind of job hundreds of times. Never any problem.'

'Good.' Mrs Pargeter took another reassuring swallow of champagne.

'Only thing is, though,' said Truffler tentatively, 'it'll cost a bit. I mean, for the courier, a few other expenses ...'

A plump hand waved away the objection. 'Don't worry. Veronica Chastaigne'll pay for all that. She seems to have unlimited money—and seems to want to spend as much of it as possible before she pops off.'

'Why do you reckon that is?'

Mrs Pargeter smiled shrewdly. 'Reading between the lines, I'd say it's so that she leaves as little of it as possible to her son.'

'Ah, right. Toby, that'd be? The accountant?'

'Mm.'

'I haven't met the young man, but I've heard about him. Haven't been that impressed by what I've heard either. Never had much time for accountants ... well, except of course for the imaginative ones ... and there are precious few of those around these days.' He gave a thoughtful nod. 'Yeah, poor old Bennie'd be well miffed if he knew Toby was, like, disowning him. After all the old man done for the boy. He was a good lad, old Bennie. Heart in the right place, no question.'

'So I've heard. Anyway, tell me, Truffler, how will the plan work?'

'Dead easy. Sweet as a nut. Gary 'n' me are set up for tomorrow night. Down to Chastaigne Varleigh with the van, Mrs Chastaigne lets us in, we load up the paintings ...'

'And where do you take them?'

'Lock-up I've got. Safe as houses—' He chuckled mournfully. 'No, darn sight safer than most houses. And then, soon as poss, we start taking the goods back to where they belong.'

'Will that be tricky?'

'Piece of cake.'

'Good. So I'll have kept my word to Veronica Chastaigne.'

'Course you will. Honour will have been satisfied.'

Mrs Pargeter raised her glass. 'Excellent,

Truffler. Let's drink to the success of the job.'

'Right.' He raised his to clink against hers. 'And let's drink to the hope that they'll all be as easy, eh?'

Chapter Twelve

'It was Bennie Logan you were talking about, wasn't it, sir?'

Inspector Wilkinson looked up from his desk with distaste. He didn't approve of junior officers bursting into his office without knocking, and he didn't like the sound of what the junior officer in question was saying. The art theft case was his; he hadn't mentioned the name of Bennie Logan to anyone. It sounded horribly as if Sergeant Hughes had been showing some initiative.

Still, ignorance was going to be the best starting position. He placed his half-smoked cigarette in the ashtray. 'I don't know what you're talking about, Hughes.'

'I've been doing some research through the files.'

'Why?'

'Well, you wouldn't tell me anything, sir, so I made it my business to find out for myself.'

'This is *my* case, Hughes. I don't like other people poking around in my business.'

The Sergeant stared defiantly into his adversary's eyes. 'There was nothing secret about it, sir. None of the files had any special security rating. They're all accessible to any member of the Force who happens to be interested in them.'

'And why do you happen to be interested in them?'

'Because I'm supposed to working with you on the bloody case and you won't tell me anything!'

Inspector Wilkinson winced at this outburst, but didn't offer a reprimand. He just looked reproachfully at his young colleague and asked, 'So what do you reckon you've found out?'

'There's a strong suggestion that Bennie Logan was behind all the robberies. He wasn't directly involved in any of them, but all of the likely perpetrators had links with him at some level. Everything seems to lead back to Chastaigne Varleigh.'

'Maybe,' said the Inspector. 'Yes, that is a possible interpretation of the facts.' He drummed his fingers on the cigarette-scarred surface of his desk. 'It must have taken you some time to go through all those files, Hughes.'

'Yes, sir.' The Sergeant yawned. 'I have been putting in the hours, actually. Up pretty late last couple of nights.'

'Hmm. You're very *keen*, aren't you?' Wilkinson was unable to keep the distaste out of his voice.

'Yes, I am, sir. I'm not ashamed of that. I want to get ahead in the Force, sir. I want to be the kind of detective who makes his mark.'

It could have been Wilkinson's younger self speaking. Of latter years he had kept quiet about such aspirations; they tended only to prompt ribaldry from his colleagues. Yes, he remembered when he had been full of ambition, just as Sergeant Hughes was now. But Wilkinson had been kept down, had his ambitions thwarted by the jealousy of older, less gifted officers.

And he was determined now to see to it that exactly the same thing happened to Sergeant Hughes.

'You haven't done any follow-up interviews with any of the witnesses, have you, Hughes?'

'No, sir. I haven't had time yet. But I was planning to talk to them when—'

Suddenly Wilkinson, moustache bristling, was on his feet and bellowing across his desk, 'You will do nothing of the kind! You will do nothing more connected with the case without telling me beforehand precisely what action you propose to take. And you will only then do it if you have my express permission. You have no idea, Hughes, of the delicacy of this operation. Its outcome can only be successful if it is conducted in absolute secrecy. If you imagine, Hughes, that I have kept the facts from you out of some kind of dog-in-the-manger selfishness, then you have a very inaccurate notion of what makes a good copper. I have kept you in the dark because I know how easily rumours can spread. The very walls have ears, you know, Hughes—even inside a police station. I am very close to tying up this case once and for all—and if the whole elaborate mechanism gets destroyed at this stage by some wet-behind-the-ears, newly promoted sergeant who fancies himself as Sherlock Holmes, I'll ... well, I won't be responsible for my actions!'

Hughes hadn't seen his boss speaking in this vein before, and it was undeniably impressive. Most of the time Inspector Wilkinson came across as an ineffectual old fuddy-duddy, a dinosaur in the Police Force, whose retirement could not come soon enough. But now, he had a certain magnificence. Here was a man who knew what he was doing, a man who was well ahead of the game, and who had all the details of the case at his fingertips. Hughes was properly subdued by the outburst.

Wilkinson sank slowly back into his chair. 'Do you take my point?'

'Yes, sir,' the Sergeant mumbled.

'Good.' The Inspector gave him a bleak smile. 'So ... since you've got as far as you have in the case, what would be your next step, Sergeant Hughes?'

'I'd apply for a search warrant and have a look around Chastaigne Varleigh.'

'Would you?'

'Yes, sir.'

'And do you imagine for a moment that I haven't thought of that?' Wilkinson reached into his desk drawer and pulled out a folded document. 'One search warrant, all duly signed and authorized.'

'Yes, sir,' the chastened Sergeant repeated.

'The only important thing now is the timing of when we go in. As I believe I may have mentioned before, Hughes, the mark of a good copper is an intuitive instinct for timing. That is something I have, and something that you may possibly over the years develop.'

The Sergeant couldn't stop himself from asking, 'So are we going in straight away, sir? When are we going in?'

'That is something that *I* will decide. I am in charge of this case, and all decisions concerning it will be taken by *me.*'

'Of course, sir. But will it be soon?'

'Yes, Hughes.' Inspector Wilkinson smiled a confident—almost complacent—smile. 'It will be very soon indeed.'

Chapter Thirteen

It was night. Diluted moonlight washed over the gravel outside Chastaigne Varleigh, where a red Transit van was parked. A thickset man jumped out of the van's back doors and said to his mate, 'Nearly done. All we got to get now is the—'

'Who's this coming?' the other man hissed, and pointed down the drive. Through the metal gates swung the headlights of another vehicle.

'Don't think we'll wait to find out!'

The two men leapt in the van's cab, and gunned its engine into life. They waited till the approaching vehicle—also a red Transit van—had drawn up just behind them, then screeched off down the drive in a fusillade of gravel.

The two men in the newly arrived van only got a quick impression of the driver's face. It was unfamiliar, heavy and sour-looking.

'Who the hell were they?' asked Truffler Mason in bewilderment.

'I don't know,' Gary replied.

'D'you get their number?'

'Course I did.' Gary's memory for number plates was photographic and infallible.

The two men jumped out of the cab and hurried towards the house.

'I don't like the look of this at all,' murmured Truffler, pulling at the chain beside the heavy oak door and setting up a distant jangling inside the house. 'Something's seriously wonky.'

'Hope nothing's happened to the old bird,' said Gary anxiously.

'No, it's all right, I can hear footsteps. She's coming.'

The door opened, and Veronica Chastaigne stood there, blinking at them in some astonishment. Outlined in the thin moonlight, she looked paler and more frail than ever. 'Good evening. Can I help you?'

'Yes. I'm Truffler Mason and this is Gary,' said Truffler. 'We've been sent by Mrs Pargeter to collect your paintings.'

The old lady's astonishment grew. 'What? But some other men have been and done that.'

'The ones who've just gone?'

'I suppose so. I didn't think they'd got all the paintings, but maybe they had.'

'Damn!' Truffler Mason looked down the drive without hope. The tail lights of the first Transit were long out of sight. 'Damn!' he repeated. 'Who the hell were they?'

The walls of the Long Gallery looked depressingly bare, their oak panelling loweringly dark. Of the rich array of paintings Mrs Pargeter had been shown, only three remained. There were a couple of minor Madonnas and a voluptuous Rubens nude.

'I'm sorry.' Veronica Chastaigne shrugged helplessly. 'I was told two men would be arriving in a red van. Two men arrived in a red van, so I naturally assumed they were the ones I was expecting.'

'Yes, of course, Mrs Chastaigne. It wasn't your fault.' Truffler shook his head in frustration as he looked around the denuded space.

Gary was equally angry. 'How did they know it was going to be a red van? Someone's got to have been talking out of turn.'

'Yes, and I'll damned well find out who—'

Truffler's words were stopped by the sound of a little sigh escaping from Veronica Chastaigne. He turned, but neither he nor Gary was quick enough to catch the old lady before she collapsed unconscious on to the wooden floor.

The chauffeur was instantly kneeling down beside her. He lifted the pitifully light form a little to cradle her head in his arms. Veronica Chastaigne gave no signs of noticing what was happening to her.

'Blimey O'Reilly! She's not dead, is she?'

'No.' Gary looked up unhappily at his colleague. 'Doesn't look too good, though.'

Chapter Fourteen

Inspector Wilkinson felt cheerful—even blithe—as Sergeant Hughes drove him along the next morning. They'd given up the Wagner experiment and were listening to a golden oldie radio station, which was much more the Inspector's style. And Hughes was properly subdued, almost deferential, in his manner. The outburst in the office, Wilkinson felt confident, had done the trick. The Sergeant now realized the kind of man he was up against.

'Did I mention, Hughes,' the Inspector mused, 'that one of the most important qualities of a good copper is patience?'

'Yes, sir, you did.'

'I've been building up this case for such a long time, you know, and it would have been so easy to rush it, to go in before everything was ready ... and that would have screwed up the whole thing.'

'Yes, sir. If we do find what we're hoping to inside the house ...'

'Hmm?'

'... what will happen? Bennie Logan's dead. He can't be charged with anything, can he?'

'No, but his wife's still alive.'

'She didn't have anything to do with the actual robberies.'

'She must've known they'd taken place. I gather she's not a stupid woman, and the kind of press coverage those robberies got ... no one could pretend they didn't know about them. No, Veronica Chastaigne definitely knew the stuff was hot.'

'So what could she be charged with?'

'Don't know exactly. Receiving stolen goods, perhaps? But don't you worry about it—we'll find something.' The Inspector chuckled in self-congratulation. 'Did I mention, Hughes, that another of the most important qualities of a good copper is a sense of timing ...?'

'Yes, you did, sir,' the Sergeant replied patiently.

It was only when they stood in the Long Gallery, looking at the naked walls, that Sergeant Hughes realized just exactly how good Inspector Wilkinson's sense of timing was.

Chapter Fifteen

Veronica Chastaigne looked very small, almost doll-like, sunken amongst the covers and pillows of the hospital bed. Around her in the private room loomed the impedimenta of serious illness—the row of monitors, the stand for the drip that disappeared into bandages round her left wrist, the cylinder of oxygen and its mask, not currently in use but standing by in ominous readiness. On top of the covers, Mrs Pargeter's plump fingers reassuringly encompassed the old lady's bony hand, as she asked gently, 'So you can't think of anyone who might have known about the paintings?'

Veronica Chastaigne shook her head forcefully, but with little strength. Her voice sounded deeply tired as she replied,

'Nobody did. Very few people ever came to the house, and none of them was allowed to see the gallery.'

'And you don't think news of the paintings' existence would have got round in ...' Mrs Pargeter paused for a moment to come up with a phrase of appropriate discretion 'the sort of circles where people might have been interested in that kind of thing ...?'

'No,' the old lady asserted firmly. 'My husband was meticulous about the "need to know" principle. He recognized the importance of keeping certain things quiet.'

'So did mine,' said Mrs Pargeter, with a momentary flicker of wistfulness.

'No. No one outside the family knew of the gallery's existence. Bennie made absolutely certain of that.'

Mrs Pargeter looked thoughtful. She remembered that Truffler Mason had heard rumours of the hidden stash of famous paintings, but didn't think it the moment to mention that. 'Well, someone knew they were there ...' she mused.

'The only person who'd been in that gallery since Bennie died—apart from Toby and myself—was you.'

'Yes.' Realizing the potential implication of the old lady's remark, Mrs Pargeter flushed. 'But surely you don't think that I would have—'

'Not you yourself, obviously, Mrs Pargeter,' said Veronica Chastaigne evenly. 'Some of your helpers, however, have in the past been involved in criminal activities.'

'I don't deny it. In the past, though. Not now. Now they're all honourable men—really. I can assure you, none of them would have broken my trust in that way.'

'I hope you're right!'

The doubt in the old lady's voice offended Mrs Pargeter, but she did not let it show. After all, if Truffler had heard rumours, maybe they were common currency in certain circles. 'What about Toby ...?' she asked diffidently.

Veronica Chastaigne was offended in her turn, and she made no attempt to hide it. 'You're not suggesting my own son might be involved in this burglary?'

'No, no,' Mrs Pargeter soothed. 'I just meant—how has he reacted to what's happened?'

The invalid's expression soured. 'I regret

to say he's delighted.' In response to a quizzical look, she went on, 'The removal of the paintings by thieves saves him what he might anticipate to be embarrassing scenes with the police after my death.'

'Ah. Yes ... So he had no idea of your plans to return the goods?'

'Good heavens, no. And, even though their disappearance in the way you and I had intended would also have let him off the hook, I'm sure he would never have given his blessing to what we were proposing to do. He has rather different moral attitudes from mine.' The thin face formed a grimace of distaste. 'Though I don't like to say it about my own son, I'm afraid in Toby I have produced an insufferable prig.'

Mrs Pargeter chuckled. 'There's no one more self-righteous than first generation straight. Like people who've just given up smoking, or reformed alcoholics.'

Through the frosted glass of the door the outline of two men in suits was visible. 'Looks like the doctor's come to check you out.' Mrs Pargeter gave the thin old hand a final pat. 'I'd better be on my way. Leave you to get some rest.'

'Yes.' Veronica Chastaigne looked suddenly more frail than ever. 'I am extraordinarily tired ...'

Leaning forward to plant a kiss on the pale cheek, Mrs Pargeter whispered, 'Don't worry, Veronica, I'll sort it out. Track down those paintings and get them back to where they should be.'

'I'm sorry to put you to so much trouble ...'

'No problem. Soon get it sorted.' Moving, as ever, daintily for someone of her bulk, Mrs Pargeter crossed to the door. 'Cheerio,' she said as she opened it.

Veronica Chastaigne raised a tired hand in farewell and seemed to sink even deeper into the bedclothes.

The two suited men who faced Mrs Pargeter in the corridor did not look like doctors. One she recognized as Veronica's son, but the other was unfamiliar to her. The suit he wore, however, had overtones of a profession other than the medical. Financial? Legal, perhaps?

Though she knew full well who Toby Chastaigne was, they had not officially met, so Mrs Pargeter just gave the two men a cheery smile and hurried off.

Toby's small eyes followed her suspiciously down the corridor until she was out of sight. Then, with a nod to his companion, he opened the door to his mother's room. 'Come on in.'

Through the slit of her drooping eyelids, Veronica Chastaigne took in the new arrivals without enthusiasm.

'Good morning, Mother,' said Toby, bending down to give her cheek the most perfunctory dusting with his lips. 'I brought my solicitor along, so that we can tie up a few loose ends ...'

Veronica Chastaigne feigned sleep.

Chapter Sixteen

Inspector Wilkinson sat alone in the unmarked car, thinking gloomy thoughts. The mistimed raid on Chastaigne Varleigh had been a body blow to him. He'd been planning the operation so long that he'd invested more hopes and ambitions than he'd realized in its successful outcome. This had been intended to be the big one, the masterstroke which wiped away the memory of so many past failures, even of the terrible moment when he had just missed entrapping the late Mr Pargeter. Proving the Chastaigne Varleigh connection to the art thefts would have ensured that Detective Inspector Craig Wilkinson had made his mark.

Except that the coup hadn't worked. The Long Gallery had been empty, although there were enough tell-tale clues—picture-hooks, rectangles of dust, outlines of darker wood where pictures had hung—to suggest it hadn't been empty for long.

Detective Inspector Craig Wilkinson was going to have to find another way to make his mark.

It was a relief to be alone in the car that morning. He was beginning to find the presence of Sergeant Hughes distinctly irksome. From the start Wilkinson had detected in the young man an unattractive cockiness, which at times bordered on disrespect. Since the Chastaigne Varleigh débâcle, the disrespect had been overt.

No, Wilkinson decided, it was a relief not to have Hughes with him (though he might have revised that opinion had he known that the Sergeant was at that moment once again immersed in files of the Inspector's old cases).

Life has dealt me a pretty lousy hand, Wilkinson thought self-pityingly. In the cop shows he watched and the crime novels he read many of the heroes had family connections to make them interesting. A crippled sibling always helped, or a child with a serious medical condition. Wives could also be very useful as a means of enriching their man's personality. A wife in an iron lung could do wonders, or one with a secret drinking problem.

And wives who had terminal illnesses or, even better, wives who were dead, could do much for a detective's sympathy rating. A dead wife in the background could leave a hero embittered, throwing himself wholeheartedly into his work so as not to have time to brood, but also available for the odd entanglement with a cleared suspect or an attractive young colleague. (These entanglements were doomed to be of short duration, but usually involved some very good sex on the way.) Yes, the right sort of deceased wife profile offered another way for a good copper to make his mark.

But Inspector Wilkinson hadn't had that kind of luck. His ex-wife was still very much alive, living in Stockport with a croupier fifteen years younger than her. She had not had any secret illnesses or agonies. Nor had their parting been a dramatic, tempestuous moment always to be regretted by one of those magnificent couples who could not live with each other but could not live without each other. No, the former Mrs Wilkinson had left her husband because she found him terminally boring.

Maybe that's what he was, the Inspector thought in a rare moment of total self-doubt. Maybe the moment that was going to salvage his career—or his whole life—was never going to happen. Maybe he was terminally boring.

But even as he reached the nadir of this dispiriting thought, it gave way to a flicker of hope. Everything wasn't all over. There was still one lead to follow up, one door imperceptibly ajar, which, if pushed with sufficient delicacy, might open up the route to a totally new area of success.

The change of mood was prompted by the sight of a woman emerging from the hospital's front gates. Broad-beamed and impressive in her bright silk print dress, she stepped daintily towards the convenient limousine which had just slid to the kerb.

Inspector Wilkinson stepped out of his car and in two or three large strides had moved across to intercept her. 'Excuse me, madam ...'

He caught the full beam of the violet-blue eyes, which showed their customary expression of puzzled innocence. 'Yes, can I help you?'

'You may recall we met the other day, when I was making enquiries about this limousine.'

'Yes, of course I remember.'

'And it struck me that on that occasion I didn't introduce myself ...'

'No.' She sounded a little mystified by this information.

'... though you did recognize—correctly —that I am a member of the Police Force.'

'Yes.'

'Well, I felt I should tell you that I am Detective Inspector Craig Wilkinson.'

'Ah. Well, thank you. A pleasure to meet you.'

Their eyes were locked. The Inspector seemed to be making a mental note of every detail of her appearance. As his scrutiny continued, Mrs Pargeter began to feel a little uneasy. Why was he so interested in her? Surely he couldn't know anything about the job she had agreed to undertake for Veronica Chastaigne?

She let out a little cough to break the impasse. 'Well, I'd better be on my way, Inspector Wilkinson.'

He stood aside. 'Of course.' She turned away towards the limousine, but his voice stopped her. 'You didn't tell me your name.'

'No, I didn't.' She faced him once again, with complete composure. 'My name is Mrs Pargeter.'

'Oh,' he said, surprised. It was a name that had very significant reverberations for Inspector Wilkinson.

'Mrs Melita Pargeter. Should you wish to contact me, I am currently residing at Greene's Hotel in Mayfair.'

'Right. And should you wish to contact me, here is my card. The mobile number is the best one to catch me on.' He handed the card across, and stood back. 'Thank you very much, Mrs Pargeter. You've been most helpful.'

His tone of voice gave her permission to continue her journey into Gary's limousine.

But, as she did so, Mrs Pargeter could feel the eyes of Inspector Wilkinson boring into her back. It gave her a slightly unpleasant *frisson*. Although her conscience was entirely clear, and she knew she had never transgressed the law in even the tiniest particular, there was still something uncomfortable about this level of interest from the Metropolitan Police.

Chapter Seventeen

She had intended to communicate her worries about the Inspector to Truffler Mason the minute he arrived at the hotel, but first she had to go through a litany of self-recrimination. Mrs Pargeter was sitting at her usual table in the bar, drinking champagne with Hedgeclipper Clinton, when Truffler shambled in, literally wringing his hands in anguish.

'I feel such a fool, such a bloody idiot, Mrs P,' he moaned, before he'd even sat down, and certainly before he'd touched his drink. 'Simple thing like shifting those pictures from Chastaigne Varleigh and I go and screw it up, let some villains ace in ahead of us and nick the lot.'

'You're sure they were villains?' asked Mrs. Pargeter, who was not showing the same reticence as her guest with the champagne. 'Sure they weren't police?'

'If they'd been on the side of the law, Mrs Chastaigne'd certainly have heard something by now. Besides, I got a look at them. They were villains all right. And,' Truffler added thoughtfully, 'villains with extremely good information.'

'What do you mean?' asked Hedge-clipper.

'They must've known we was about to raid the place.'

'How can you be so sure?'

'The timing's too much of a coincidence. If they'd been casing the joint, or if they was acting on a tip-off from one of Bennie Logan's cronies, they could've done it any time in the five years since he died. But no, they chose the very day we'd planned to lift the loot. They knew something.'

Hedgeclipper Clinton nodded. It made sense.

'I don't like it,' said Truffler. 'It's like being back in the days of Posey Narker.'

'Yes, it is. Not nice.'

'I'm sorry?' said Mrs Pargeter guilelessly. 'Did you say "Posey Narker"?'

'Yes.' Truffler rubbed his chin in pained recollection. 'Fact is, while your husband was alive, we had a bit of trouble with information ending up where it shouldn't.'

'Oh?'

'Seemed like someone Mr Pargeter trusted was betraying that trust. Police kept knowing more than they should have known about things that were about to happen. Never found out who the grass was. All we got, from one of our informants inside the Met, was this name—"Posey Narker". Clearly someone's idea of a joke. Annoying, though, because we knew the grass was like, teasing us, sending us up, challenging us to catch him. We never did, though. Which was lucky for him,' Truffler concluded darkly.

'Too right.' Hedgeclipper Clinton was transformed for a moment from hotel manager to an earlier, more aggressive persona. 'I had a few plans for the little rat if we ever had got hold of him ...'

'Anyway, we're talking a long time ago,' said Truffler, closing the subject. 'This business of the villains being tipped off and getting in before us at Chastaigne

Varleigh ... well, it, like, reminded me of Posey Narker, that's all.'

Mrs Pargeter reverted to a point she'd made earlier. 'You are absolutely sure the ones you describe as villains had nothing to do with the police?'

Truffler Mason looked up sharply at the intonation of her words. 'Yes, of course I'm sure. But why do you say that? Have you got some inside info?'

'Not exactly,' replied Mrs Pargeter, now able to get on to the subject she'd wanted to start with. 'There's this Detective Inspector who seems to be sniffing around.'

Truffler was instantly alert. 'Sniffing around? How d'you mean?'

'I first met him that afternoon I'd gone to your office, you know, to tell you about what Veronica Chastaigne had asked me to do.'

'Yes?'

'He had some enquiry about Gary's limousine. Said it'd been seen near a crime scene in Tulse Hill. Well, Gary's not been to Tulse Hill in ages, so clearly somebody'd misidentified the car. I didn't think any more about it ... until I found the same policeman waiting outside the hospital this morning after I'd been visiting

116

Veronica Chastaigne.'

Hedgeclipper Clinton looked alarmed, and Truffler Mason's long body was rigid with tension. 'A detective inspector you said?'

'That's right,' Mrs Pargeter confirmed.

The hotel manager licked his lips nervously, but let Truffler continue putting the questions. 'What did he ask you about today?'

'Well, that was what was odd,' replied Mrs Pargeter. 'Nothing, really.'

'Nothing?'

'No. It was just like he was, kind of, keeping tabs on me, monitoring my movements. Somehow he knew I'd gone to the hospital. I even get the feeling he knew he was going to meet me coming out of your office that first time. I don't like it.'

'Nor do I,' Truffler agreed whole-heartedly. 'I wonder ...'

'Wonder what?' asked Hedgeclipper, with another flick of the tongue around his dry lips.

'Well, maybe sneaking the stuff from Chastaigne Varleigh was a police set-up ... Maybe they're working on some kind of major entrapment plan ...' His huge

117

head shook slowly from side to side. 'No, I don't like this at all, Hedgeclipper.'

'Nor me.'

'I mean, personally I've nothing against the police,' said Mrs Pargeter, magnanimous as ever, 'in their place. They do a wonderful job, this country would be a much poorer place without them ... but the fact remains, I don't like them snooping around me.'

'Nor do I,' said Truffler again.

'Not,' she hastened to add, 'that I've ever done anything to arouse their interest, in a professional way. But the people they tend to recruit are not always the brightest, and one would hate for there to be any misunderstandings, for them to get the wrong end of the stick, either about me ... or about any of the people I associate with.'

'One would hate that very much indeed.' Hedgeclipper Clinton nodded agreement with the sentiment. Grimly, Truffler Mason rubbed his long chin, and said again, 'I don't like the sound of this one little bit. I'd better investigate it further.' He stood up, leaving the remainder of his champagne untouched. 'You haven't got the bloke's name, by any chance, have you?'

'Yes,' said Mrs Pargeter. 'It's Detective Inspector Craig Wilkinson.'

There was a moment's silence while Truffler and Hedgeclipper took this in. Then a snort of laughter erupted from the hotel manager. Truffler Mason's entire body shook, as he sat back down in his chair and picked up his champagne glass. He made as if to take a swig, but was laughing too much to complete the action.

'What is it?' asked Mrs Pargeter, unused to seeing that lugubrious face incapable with merriment. 'What is it that's so funny? Do I gather you two know this gentleman?'

Hedgeclipper Clinton could only nod, unable to form words but, through gasps of laughter, Truffler Mason managed to say, 'Oh, yes, I know him. I know him all right. Your husband knew him, and all, Mrs P. I'm surprised Mr Pargeter never mentioned old "Craggy" Wilkinson to you.'

'You know my husband never spoke to me about his work,' she said primly.

'No, I know he didn't as a general rule, but with old Craggy I'm surprised he could keep it to himself.'

'Why?'

'Well, some of the things he done ... they were just such good stories. You know, when me and the boys was working with your husband, whenever we needed a good laugh, we'd just tell another Craggy Wilkinson story. Isn't that right, Hedgeclipper?'

The hotel manager was sufficiently recovered to let out a 'Yes,' but the sound of the emergent word only set him off again.

'Why? What kind of things did he do?'

'Well, let's take for instance ...' Truffler paused for a moment, shuffling through a mental filing cabinet, spoiled for choice as to which anecdote he should produce first. 'All right. Try this for starters.'

Chapter Eighteen

'There was a job up Ponder's End,' said Truffler. 'Bullion delivery, very hush-hush, transfer of a load of gold ingots from some arms deal a bunch of North London villains'd done with Nigeria. Mr P'd got word of it from a baggage handler at Heathrow. Goods were going to come into the country, you see, in crates marked "Tribal Artefacts", but everyone at the airport had been bunged a bit to keep a blind eye. The baggage handler who snitched reckoned the bung wasn't big enough and he'd get a better deal from your husband. Which of course he did. Always the soul of generosity your old man was, Mrs P.

'Anyway, like as ever, the planning of the job was meticulous. Never left any angle uncovered, Mr P didn't, sorted through everything, done dry runs, rehearsals, double-checks. Any operation he was involved in was always sweet as a nut and tight as a noose.' A wistful, nostalgic look came into Truffler's eyes. 'He was an artist, your husband, Mrs P, a true artist.

'Right, so the whole thing's planned. The lorry with its crate of "Tribal Artefacts" is meant to be going from Heathrow to, like, Epping Forest where the gang's going to stash it for a couple of weeks before it gets melted down and redistributed in the form of chunky identity bracelets.

'Except, of course, it's never going to make it to Epping Forest, because in

Ponder's End it's going to be diverted from its original course. And somehow the crates of "Tribal Artefacts" are going to end up in a refrigerated ice cream lorry heading due south for Penge where the ingots will end up in far more deserving pockets than those of the North London mob.

'OK, it's all set, and then, like two days before the flight's due, Mr P gets a tip-off that the cops are on to it. Heaven knows who they got their information from. Could've been that the baggage handler was hoping to treble up his take by getting a pay-off from the filth too ... though I still think it had the hallmarks of our friend Posey Narker.

'Anyway, Jukebox Jarvis is doing a routine check when ... Oh, you don't know Jukebox Jarvis, do you, Mrs P? He was your late husband's computer expert, and, before any job, he always, like, hacked into the Metropolitan Police's computer just to see if they was on to anything.'

'Wasn't that very difficult?' asked Mrs Pargeter.

'Not for Jukebox, no. Well, there was a six-letter security password which the cops changed every day, but since they usually alternated between "police" and "secret",

Jukebox never had too much trouble.

'Anyway, like I said, this time we find the filth are on to us. A lot of detail they've got—time of the flight, what the crates are labelled, where the lorry's meant to be going, and the exact bit of Ponder's End where the hijacking's going to take place. They even know we're planning to take the loot off in an ice cream lorry. And we also find out that the officer in charge of the investigation is one Detective Inspector Craig Wilkinson.

'First time any of us has heard of him, but all right, forewarned is forearmed, your husband makes alternative arrangements. Not major changes—just intercepting the lorry the other side of Ponder's End, nearer to Heathrow, so that the deed's been done before we get to the bit where, the computer says, the police'll be waiting for us.

'So, as usual, everything goes like it should. Loot gets transferred to the ice cream lorry, ice cream lorry goes down to Penge as per arrangement, where it loses itself and its contents are satisfactorily redistributed.

'It's only later we discover what Inspector Wilkinson's done. He's only stopped another ice cream lorry and impounded it in the lock-up underneath Paddington Green Police Station. He's only arrested the driver and his mate and spent two days questioning them. Not surprisingly, they didn't have a lot to tell him. But while they're up in the interview rooms, the refrigeration's off in the lorry downstairs and its back doors have been left open and, like, next time anyone from the station has a look, they find the whole of the lock-up's awash with melted ice cream.' Truffler Mason chuckled fondly at the recollection. 'You know, Paddington Green still smells of raspberry ripple.

'So, anyway, Mrs P, that was your late husband's first encounter with Inspector Wilkinson. And from the very start, he realized what we were up against was a one-hundred per cent, copper-bottomed dumbo.'

Truffler Mason may have finished his anecdote, but Hedgeclipper Clinton had been waiting for some time to chip in with his own recollections of the unfortunate Wilkinson. 'Then there was that other time,' he said, the moment Truffler paused for breath, 'that Hampstead Music Museum job. Only a small place it was, full of biographical memorabilia from various composers, but amongst all the stuff it got was some really nice instruments, violins mostly. One Amati and a couple of Stradivariuses—and a Stradivarius cello. Well, Mrs P, as you'll remember, your old man always was a great music-lover ... and, besides, he recognized that that lot's got quite a good resale value.

'So, once again, the whole thing's set up beautifully. Times the curator and his staff go on and off duty checked out. Keyhole Crabbe's brought in—you remember him, locks and alarms specialist—and he checks out the security system. Finds the best thing to do is set up a little electronic jiggery-pokery that reverses the alarms—like, when they're switched on, the doors open silently; when they're switched off and a door's touched, all hell breaks loose. Dead simple.

'Anyway, couple of days before the lift, Jukebox Jarvis does his routine hack into Scotland Yard, and blow me if he doesn't discover that they're on to this one too.'

'Now that I'm sure was Posey Narker,' said Truffler.

'Probably. Anyway, we find out they're on to us and, what's more, the detective in charge of the case is once again—Inspector Wilkinson.

'Obviously, Mr P and everyone else is dead chuffed to hear this, and the plans for the job are adjusted accordingly. Cut a long story short, the instruments are all successfully liberated from their cases before old Craggy Wilkinson gets there. And he ends up spending the whole weekend locked in the museum. Not sure whether he knew much about music before, but by the time he got out, he could certainly tell his Arne from his Elgar!'

While Hedgeclipper chuckled at his witticism, Truffler Mason was quick to pick up the conversational baton. 'Well, by now it had become a pattern. Wilkinson was entirely reliable. Whatever he had to do, we could guarantee he'd screw it up. One time he was even duped into letting us use a Panda as a getaway car. With a police driver, and all!

'As you can imagine, Mrs P, your late husband saw the potential advantages of all this. Soon, whenever we'd got a big job coming up, he'd get Jukebox Jarvis not only to hack into the police computer for information, but to make a few changes to what he found in there. Particularly in the business of duty rosters. Jukebox'd fix it so that any time we'd got a real biggie, Detective Inspector Craig Wilkinson would be slated to be in charge of the case. Then we knew nothing could go wrong. I tell you, if Wilkinson hadn't been around, the information Posey Narker was spilling could've caused a lot more trouble than it actually did. Your husband used to say that old Craggy Wilkinson was his lucky mascot.'

Again Truffler Mason roared with laughter at the recollection, and Hedgeclipper Clinton joined him. Their laughter rose to a merry crescendo, then trickled away.

Both realizing at the same time that they had heard little for some time from the third person present in the bar, they looked across at her. On Mrs Pargeter's soft, creamy brow was a wrinkle of puzzlement, and even a hint of reproach. 'I'm sorry,' she said. 'I'm afraid I didn't understand a single word of what you were talking about.'

Truffler Mason and Hedgeclipper Clinton fell over themselves in their confusion and assurances that they couldn't think what'd come over them, that they'd been well out of order, that they didn't wish in any way to imply that the late Mr Pargeter had at any level been connected with any activity which did not fit within the strictest parameters of the British legal system.

Eventually Mrs Pargeter inclined her head, gracefully accepting their apologies.

'All we were really saying,' said Truffler Mason plaintively, 'is that if Inspector Wilkinson's sniffing around you, you have absolutely nothing to worry about.'

'Thank you.' But the puzzlement hadn't entirely left Mrs Pargeter's innocent face. 'I can't imagine why it took you so long to tell me that.' She smiled easily, letting them off the hook. 'Now, did you say HRH and I were going to see Palings Price tomorrow ...?'

Chapter Nineteen

They were once again in the back room of 'DENZIL PRICE INTERIORS'. Propped up on a minimalist steel chair was the Rubens that the thieves had left at Chastaigne Varleigh. Against the wall stood the two minor Madonnas which had also escaped abduction. The rich colours of the paintings spoiled the room's monochrome image, but the designer didn't seem to mind.

Mrs Pargeter and Hamish Ramon Henriques looked on in respectful silence while he made his expert assessment.

An expression of almost gastronomic relish played around Palings Price's mouth as he gazed at the painting. He wasn't quite licking his lips, but very nearly.

'Now this is very beautiful ...' he murmured.

'Yes ...' Mrs Pargeter agreed mistily. She had felt a great warmth for the fake Rubens in VVO's studio, but the sight of the real thing was even more potent. The painting's voluptuous flesh glowed down the centuries and found a welcoming glow in her own voluptuous flesh. Like called to like. Mrs Pargeter felt a sudden pang of sorrow that her husband was dead. The late Mr Pargeter would have really responded to that painting. It embodied everything he had ever looked for in a woman.

Maybe it was the conversation with Truffler and Hedgeclipper at Greene's

Hotel the evening before that had set her mind on the track, but she found she'd been thinking a lot about her husband that morning. Not morbid thoughts. No, rather she had a little bubble of excitement inside her, gratitude for the wonderful years that they'd had together, and a great sense of well-being. The last shadow of disappointment about the failure to get the paintings from Chastaigne Varleigh had passed. Now she felt entirely confident that Veronica Chastaigne's request would be fulfilled, and it was stimulating to be a part of the operation that would fulfil it. Mrs Pargeter felt free and irresponsible, almost skittish.

'One of the best examples of Rubens's mature period,' Palings Price was saying. 'The model was his second wife Hélène Fourment.'

'It's stunning,' Mrs Pargeter agreed. 'My husband would really have loved it.'

'Why particularly?' asked HRH.

'Well, obviously, because he liked his women—' But no. She checked herself. That was private. 'This was the sort of thing he liked,' she concluded lightly.

'Oh. Right.'

Mrs Pargeter felt the need to move

the conversation hastily on. 'Where was it stolen from?'

'Pantheon Gallery, Berne. In 1982,' said Palings Price. He pointed to the Madonnas. 'Those two were taken at the same time. Big fuss when it happened. All over the international press.'

'I'll bet it was.'

HRH ran a thoughtful hand through his splendid moustache. 'Odd that the three paintings the thieves left at Chastaigne Varleigh should be from the same haul ...'

'Yes.' Mrs Pargeter seized on the thought. 'Suggests they knew quite a lot about what they were dealing with.'

But Palings Price, who was after all an expert in these matters, was unconvinced. 'Not necessarily,' he said. 'Could just be coincidence.'

'Hmm.' Mrs Pargeter sighed a contented little sigh. 'We'll probably know more when Truffler's tracked down the rest of the stuff that was stolen.'

'You sound very confident that he'll find it.'

'Well, of course he will, Palings. Truffler's the best in the business, isn't he?'

'That's true.'

Mrs Pargeter looked again at the paintings. 'Well, at least we've got these three, so we can make a start. Do you reckon there's going to be any problem getting these back to where they came from, HRH?'

The travel agent's magnificent mane of white hair shook confidently. 'No. Berne'll be easy. Fritzi the Finger's based in Salzburg. Your husband got him out of a few spots. He'll be honoured to help, won't he, Palings?'

'Absolutely. This sort of job's meat and drink to him, anyway.'

HRH was thoughtful for a moment. 'No, the only problem will be finding a courier to get the goods out of this country ...'

'Couldn't I do that?' Mrs. Pargeter volunteered eagerly.

It was just her skittish mood of the morning finding expression, but the suggestion clearly shocked Hamish Ramon Henriques. There was a strong tone of disapproval in his voice as he said, 'I wouldn't want you to put yourself at any risk, Mrs Pargeter.'

'Besides,' the gallery owner interposed, 'smuggling old masters is actually a criminal activity ...'

'Oh yes.' She was properly contrite. 'Sorry, I got carried away there.'

Palings Price continued to spell out the situation for her. 'And you've never been personally involved in anything illegal, have you?'

An innocent blush suffused her cheeks at the very idea. 'Good heavens, no,' said Mrs Pargeter.

Chapter Twenty

The studio of VVO still looked as cluttered, but this time Mrs Pargeter was aware of how *hygienic* all of its clutter was. Having met the houseproud Deirdre Winthrop, she could no longer believe in the reality of the husband's bohemianism. The studio now appeared to her like a stage set, its dust neatly scattered, its cobwebs recently sprayed on. Even the splashes and splodges of paint on every surface no longer looked random; their exact positioning and their precise level of exuberance had been carefully calculated.

Since his last encounter with Mrs

Pargeter and HRH, VVO had been busy—though not as busy as he'd have had to be if all the pictures from Chastaigne Varleigh had been saved. The fruits of his labour were there to be seen, but this time there was no fake Rubens flesh to excite charming comparisons. What VVO had been busy on was his own work, the kind of paintings which he believed he had been placed on this earth to produce.

'Oh dear,' thought Mrs Pargeter, as she looked at the latest creations. There were three of them. In one a lamb with a watermelon grin, wearing a pink bow whose wingspan would not have shamed a jumbo jet, cavorted in front of a quaint windmill. On the second, two lovable ducklings skidded hopelessly on an icy lake, trying to catch up with the mother and the rest of her family procession. And in the third—returning to one of the artist's favourite themes—a winsome Scottie dog in a natty little tartan coat circled a blossom-laden tree, from whose branches a fluffy white pussy cat grinned down cheekily.

Two of the paintings were already fixed into aluminium frames, and VVO was easing the Scottie dog into the third.

Empty, propped against the wall, stood the finely wrought wooden frames of the Rubens and the two Madonnas.

'There,' said VVO, as he screwed the last crosspiece into position at the back of the canvas.

Palings Price looked admiringly at the framed Scottie. 'Great. And no one would ever know there was a Rubens under that piece of ...' Discretion intervened and his words trailed away.

'Under that piece of what?' asked VVO suspiciously.

'Under that piece of very fine modern painting,' said Mrs Pargeter, ever the conciliator. 'I think is what Palings was about to say, isn't that right?'

'Oh. Yes. Of course,' the interior designer lied.

VVO didn't seem entirely convinced by the cover-up. 'After I'm dead, you know,' he said truculently, 'the true value of my work will be recognized.'

'Yes, VVO, I'm sure it will,' Mrs Pargeter agreed, her soothing tone disguising the ambiguity of her words.

VVO was reassured, anyway. 'Thank you, Mrs Pargeter. At least you recognize what I'm capable of.'

'Oh, certainly.' And before the painter had time to spot another double-edged compliment, she rubbed her hands together with relish and said, 'Great, terrific. So all we need now is a courier to get the paintings down to Berne ...'

VVO looked hopefully round the room until his glance engaged with Mrs Pargeter's. She did feel tempted to give in to the appeal in those dog-like eyes. The skittish mood was still with her. The courier job wasn't complicated. Surely VVO couldn't mess it up. And the late Mr Pargeter had been renowned for constantly opening up new opportunities for his staff, trusting them with ever greater responsibilities.

But her indulgent fantasies were interrupted by the voice of Hamish Ramon Henriques. Shaking his head decidedly, the travel agent pronounced a firm 'No.'

'Oh, come on,' the artist wheedled, 'you could let me do this. It's not fair, I'm never allowed to do any of the exciting stuff. And it'd be so easy for me to be your courier. Me and Deirdre could be going off in the camper for a continental holiday. Why not? it's something we often do.'

But that suggestion prompted another

shake of HRH's fine Iberian head. 'I said no. Apart from anything else, it's always a risk entrusting this kind of thing to someone with a criminal record. The police are—'

Fury burned in the eye of VVO 'Now hang on a minute. Just because you've got a criminal record, there's no need to imagine—'

'How dare you!' HRH snapped back. 'I can assure you I do not have—'

Mrs Pargeter raised her hands as if to smooth out a lumpy duvet. 'Please, please. There's no need to argue. I'm sure no one in this room has any kind of criminal record.'

VVO and HRH looked a little sheepish after their outburst, and Palings Price's face was fixed in a rictus of self-righteousness. Mrs Pargeter gave a reassuring smile to all of them. 'Good. See, no worries on that score.'

'No,' HRH agreed, eager to sweep the disagreement hastily under the carpet. 'Your late husband took enormous care of the people who worked for him.'

Palings Price gave a nostalgic nod. 'Oh yes. You know, I was just thinking, Mrs Pargeter ...'

'Yes?'

'... what a fine man your husband was ...'

'Thank you.'

'And, you know,' the interior designer went on, 'one of the wonderful things about him was the way he encouraged the people who worked for him by always giving them new challenges, offering them the chance to do something a little different ...'

This so closely echoed Mrs Pargeter's recent thoughts that she found herself nodding. Even HRH said, 'He was excellent at that, I agree.'

'So ...' Palings Price went on, 'I think we should follow his example ...'

'By doing what?' asked Mrs Pargeter.

'By letting Vincent Vin Ordinaire be our courier.'

'Oh, please!' the painter squealed, though the expression on HRH's face, which had been moving towards the conciliatory, had quickly changed and was now far from endorsing the suggestion.

Palings Price gestured to the three aluminium-framed pieces of artwork. 'I'm sure VVO's capable of getting these three ...' another word hovered on his lips, but he managed in time to convert it to '*paintings* down to Fritzi in Berne.'

Hamish Ramon Henriques shook his head dubiously. 'I'm not sure that—'

But Palings Price had the bit between his teeth and was not to be deflected. 'Don't be such a fuddy-duddy, HRH. If Mr Pargeter hadn't given you your chance, you'd still be working for—' —the travel agent tried to interrupt, but he was too late—'London Transport,' the art dealer concluded implacably.

HRH turned away in shame, effectively handing the victory to Palings Price. 'So I think we should definitely give VVO the chance to be the courier for once.' He turned to face their late employer's widow. 'What do you say, Mrs Pargeter?'

She was torn. Caution told her that Hamish Ramon Henriques was in the right, but her natural generosity drew her towards the idea of giving VVO a break. And the thoughts she'd been entertaining about her husband suggested that he might have been inclined towards indulgence.

'Please, please!' the painter begged. 'You won't regret your decision. I'll do the job perfectly, I promise.'

Mrs Pargeter was not a weak or vacillating woman, and in this instance her natural big-heartedness did not allow her to hesitate for long. 'Oh, very well,' she said. 'You be our courier, VVO.'

'Yippee!' The painter punched the air with delight, and did a little jig around the clutter of his studio. Mrs Pargeter looked at Palings Price and saw how pleased he was by what she'd said. But she avoided the eye of Hamish Ramon Henriques. She had a feeling his view might be rather different.

Chapter Twenty-One

Inspector Wilkinson sat in the passenger seat of the unmarked car, chewing the end of his pencil. A police notebook lay open on his lap in front of him, but so far only one line had been written. As a line, he quite liked it, but it was writing a second, and a third, and a fourth that was proving difficult. Wasn't there any word in the English language that rhymed with 'ample'?

Be simpler if he came from the North. Then presumably he could use 'sample' or 'example', with short 'a's. But that wouldn't be right. He didn't know much about poetry, but he did know neither of those would be a true rhyme. And he had to make his first poem a presentable one. A good copper doesn't cut corners, even when he's writing poetry.

Inspector Wilkinson had never actually met a police officer who wrote poetry— outside of crime fiction—but he was sure there must be some. Maybe that was the way he'd make his mark in the Force, by showing his more spiritual, creative side. Yes, it was rather appealing, the image of himself, Craig Wilkinson, as a sensitive aesthete, even as the New Man perhaps.

Women went for that kind of stuff, apart from anything else. Poets never had any difficulty getting women to go to bed with them. And because they were dealing with poets, the women didn't expect anything like commitment or fidelity. They knew poets lived on far too high a plane to be sidetracked by details like that. Yes, Wilkinson thought to himself, I think I could have rather a good future as a poet (and forget the New Man bit of it).

But not until I can find something to rhyme with 'ample', he was reminded as his eye caught sight of the notebook. There's always a bloody snag, isn't there? Maybe it's the word 'ample' that needs changing, he wondered. It suits the rhythm of the line perfectly, but perhaps there's something else that would fit in as well.

He tried to think of some synonyms for 'ample'. 'Generous' ...? That was close, but it hadn't got quite the same resonance. 'Strapping' ...? Good for rhymes, but it wasn't right for anything else. 'Huge' ...? No. 'Fat' ...? No, no, no. 'Enormous' ...? Now this was getting silly.

No way round it, 'ample' was the only word. It had to be 'ample'. But ... Suddenly a memory came from his schooldays, an echo of something his English master had said, half-listened to and unheeded until this moment. 'Shakespeare wrote all of his greatest plays in blank verse, and blank verse does not rhyme.'

That's it. Wilkinson seized on the idea with delight. Poetry doesn't have to rhyme! He looked down again at the notebook for a moment, but his glee was short-lived. The second line still didn't leap out at him. He couldn't think of a single thing he wanted to say.

God, he thought, this poetry lark's

bloody difficult. There must be easier ways in which I can make my mark. Maybe I should have a go at exotic sandwich-making or serial adultery instead ...?

'What's that then?' Wilkinson was so abstracted by his thoughts that a curious Sergeant Hughes was in the driver's seat beside him before he'd noticed.

'Oh, nothing. I was just, er, pulling together some of the threads of the case.' The Inspector hastened to shove the notebook back in his pocket.

But he hadn't been quick enough. Hughes had caught sight of a word. 'What's "curvaceous" got to do with the case then, sir?'

'Mind your own business, Sergeant. A good copper frequently takes an oblique approach to a subject. It rarely pays to go for the obvious. Lateral thinking is what you need in our line of work.' Then, in a tone of professional grumpiness, he asked, 'Anyway, what kept you? You were due here half an hour ago.'

'Sorry, sir.'

'You haven't answered my question. I asked what kept you. What have you been doing, Hughes? Where have you been?'

'I was just doing a bit more research, sir.'

'Research, eh? Into what?'

'Into this case, sir. The case we're working on.'

Wilkinson's eyes narrowed with distaste. 'I thought I'd warned you about going out on a limb, Hughes. Never forget who's in charge of this case. I am.'

'I'm well aware of that, sir, but I just thought, you know, two heads are better than one.'

'A very dangerous supposition, Hughes. And one that certainly does not always prove to be correct. It depends entirely on the quality of the heads involved.'

'Listen, sir. I've just been going through the old files again.'

'Looking for what?'

'Connections, sir.'

'What kind of connections?'

'Connections between some of the names involved in the case. You know, seeing who reports to who, who's worked with who, looking for links, piecing together the network. Do you understand the kind of thing I mean, sir?'

Wilkinson let out a long, weary sigh. He had spent most of his professional career going through exactly the process Sergeant Hughes had just described. 'And have you reached any conclusions?' he asked in a pained voice.

'Well, assuming we're right about the stolen paintings having been at Chastaigne Varleigh, then that immediately means that Bennie Logan has to have been involved. Now, amongst people he'd worked with in the past was an art thief called Fritzi the Finger, who works out of Salzburg.'

'And?' asked Wilkinson, trying to keep the annoyance out of his voice. It had taken him three years to work out the connection between Bennie Logan and Fritzi the Finger; Hughes appeared to have done it in as many days.

'*And,* sir, both of them had occasional connections with a certain criminal master-mind.'

'Who was that?' The Inspector's voice shrivelled under its own sarcasm. 'Professor Moriarty?'

'No, sir, it was a man who's now dead, but who in his time was behind some of the biggest criminal operations in London. His name was Mr Pargeter.'

'Really?' Wilkinson tried to keep his voice as casual and uninterested as possible, but the name still brought him an unwelcome *frisson*.

'Yes, sir. I'm building up a dossier on his activities. The late Mr Pargeter, so far as I can tell, was a great coordinator. He knew all kinds of specialists in the underworld and his skill was in getting them together. He was the brains behind everything, but his influence reached out to a whole army of minor villains.'

'Why're you telling me all this, Hughes?'

'Because if you entrap someone like Mr Pargeter, sir, you don't just get one villain, you get a whole pack of them. Apparently, I read in the files, at one stage there was a police initiative to get him, but it was conducted so incompetently that—'

'Yes, yes,' Inspector Wilkinson interrupted testily. 'There's one thing you seem to be ignoring in all this extremely fascinating conversation, and that is that you're talking about someone who is dead. I'm sure it would be entirely possible to set up a very clever operation to entrap Mr Pargeter, but you'd be ten years too late.'

'Mr Pargeter may be dead, sir,' the Sergeant said slowly, 'but his influence didn't die with him.'

'What're you saying, Hughes?'

'I'm saying that Mr Pargeter's network still exists.'

'I see.' The Inspector smiled sceptically. 'And who, may I ask, runs this mythical organization?'

'His widow.'

'Who?'

'His widow. Mrs Pargeter.' Wilkinson gaped, and Hughes pressed home his advantage. 'What is more, I have now established that, on the third day we worked together doing surveillance at Chastaigne Varleigh, she was the woman who arrived at the house by limousine.'

'What!'

'I've checked it out.' The Sergeant was now having difficulty keeping a note of smugness out of his voice. He'd really got the old dinosaur on the run now. 'That woman's name was Mrs Pargeter.'

There was a silence, then inspector Wilkinson broke it with a patronizing chuckle. 'Hughes, Hughes, Hughes,' he said pityingly, 'what it must be still to have the boundless enthusiasm of youth.'

'What do you mean, sir?'

'I mean that you have no basis for assuming that the woman who entered Chastaigne Varleigh has anything to do

147

with the late Mr Pargeter.'

'But of course I have. For heaven's sake, she's got the same surname!'

'Yes, and so the obvious thing to do would be to assume that they're related.'

'Seems reasonable to me, sir.'

'Yes, it probably does to *you*, Hughes, but what distinguishes an exceptional copper from a run-of-the-mill copper is the ability to see beyond the obvious. Sometimes, you know, we can learn from the world of crime fiction. Have you read any of Conan Doyle's Sherlock Holmes stories, Hughes?'

'No. I'm more interested in real-life crime than that kind of hokum.'

'Oh, don't be hasty, Hughes. You'd be very unwise to dismiss Sherlock Holmes as hokum. The important lesson he offers to every real-life copper is that one shouldn't look for the obvious. Are you familiar with *The curious incident of the dog in the night-time?*'

'No,' the Sergeant replied sullenly.

'Well, you should be. I mean, what would you expect a dog to do in the night-time?'

'Sleep?'

'Yes. Or bark.'

'It'd only bark if something disturbed it.'

'Exactly, Hughes, exactly! You know, you might have the makings of a half-decent cop yet,' Wilkinson conceded generously. 'In the relevant Sherlock Holmes story, it's what the dog *doesn't* do that's important. The reader's expectations are reversed—therein lies Conan Doyle's cunning. And it's just the same in this case. Mrs Pargeter has the same surname as the late Mr Pargeter—and that is the very reason why they're *not* related.'

'So are you going to leave it like that, sir? Assume they're not related without even checking?'

'No, no, Hughes,' the Inspector replied patiently as if to an over-excited five-year-old. 'Of course I'll check it out. A good copper always checks things out. But I'll be very surprised if my instinct isn't proved right once again. You'll see, Hughes—and hopefully you'll learn too, eh?'

'Yes, sir,' Hughes replied sullenly.

'Remember what I said. It rarely pays to go for the obvious. Lateral thinking is what you need in our line of work.'

Inspector Wilkinson grinned complacently. Sergeant Hughes seethed.

Chapter Twenty-Two

Gary's limousine sighed to a halt outside an ordinary-looking terrace in a North London suburb. Even though this was not a commercial booking and his passenger was only Truffler Mason, force of habit made the chauffeur get out and open the back door. Everyone who travelled in one of Gary's cars got the same first-class treatment.

'Thanks, mate,' said Truffler, and looked up at the house. 'He'll be good on this stuff, Gary. He's great on computers, but anything to do with motors, I always go to Jukebox Jarvis too. You know him?'

Gary opened the gate and they walked up the short path to the front door. It only took one and a quarter of Truffler's huge strides. 'I've heard of him, obviously,' said the chauffeur, 'not met him. One thing I've always wanted to know, though, was why he was called "Jukebox".'

Truffler Mason lifted the Lincoln Imp doorknocker and let it fall. 'Because he was Mr Pargeter's archivist.'

'Archivist? But I still don't get—'

Patiently, Truffler spelled it out. 'Because he kept the records.'

'Oh,' said Gary. 'Right.'

The door opened to reveal a small, balding, inoffensive man in a homely cardigan. Behind thick glasses, his eyes sparkled as he recognized one of his visitors.

'Truffler!' he cried, seizing the tall man's hand. 'How you doing, me old kipper?'

Jukebox Jarvis's office was in his front room, a tangled maze of computers, monitors, printers, modems and scanners, all interconnected in a lunatic cat's cradle of cables. So extensive was the array of hardware that it was impossible to see the tables and filing cabinets on which the equipment rested.

The only objects in the room which weren't computer-related hung on the walls. They were sentimental animal pictures of quite mesmerizing awfulness. The level of winsomeness among their fluffy chicks and simpering Scotties made VVO's daubs look like models of classical restraint.

Jukebox Jarvis clearly knew all the short cuts of his computer system. A few clicks of the mouse and he had found the relevant information bank.

'You're sure it's a red Ford Transit we're looking for?' he asked.

'Certain,' said Gary. 'Because we was driving the same model. Remember thinking when I saw it—well, there's a coincidence.'

'No coincidence really,' Truffler pointed out, 'when you come to think of it, because we was both intending to load up with the same goods. And Mrs Chastaigne had been told to expect a red Transit.'

'Yeah, but we didn't know that at the time.'

Truffler Mason let out a hollow laugh. 'No. Otherwise we'd have stopped them then and there, got the loot and saved Jukebox all this hassle.'

The computer buff airily waved away the suggestion of inconvenience. 'It's no bother, really, Truffler, me old kipper. Never have any problem hacking into the police's vehicle records.' He chuckled. 'Sometimes a bit trickier to get into their system on a murder enquiry, mind you …'

'I'm not surprised.'

'... but I usually manage it,' said Jukebox Jarvis with a complacent smile. 'Always nice to know how far the Plod are behind amateur investigations, isn't it?'

'Very useful,' Truffler agreed. 'And in the old days used to be handy knowing how up to speed they were on the next little job Mr Pargeter had in mind. And how much info Posey Narker had given them.'

'Yeah. Happy days, they was, eh? Happy days.' Jukebox Jarvis sighed, but then giggled. 'Incidentally, I heard about that case you done for Mrs Pargeter. You know, when you nailed the blokes who'd killed Willie Cass. I gather you gave the police a full report on that and just told them who needed arresting.'

'Well ...' Truffler smiled modestly. 'I suppose they might have got there in their own time, but, quite honestly, did anyone want to wait that long?'

Jukebox Jarvis looked back at his screen, where the cursor blinked, demanding information. 'Now, Gary, the number of the van ...?'

The chauffeur placed his fingertips on his temples, screwed up his eyes and concentrated fiercely. 'Yeah,' he said after a moment. 'I've nearly got it.'

The other two watched as he went into a state that was almost trance-like. 'Must be great having a photographic memory,' Jukebox whispered to Truffler.

'Isn't really that,' the investigator whispered back. 'It's training. Mr Pargeter taught him the techniques, so whenever Gary went out on a job he'd automatically make a mental note of any registrations that might be suspicious.'

'Right.'

Gary's eyes suddenly flashed open and he announced the relevant registration.

'Great.' Jukebox Jarvis keyed in the information. 'You reckon we should be looking for hijack and theft of red Transits or just straight ownership, Truffler?'

'Start with the owners. Depends who the thieves was. If they didn't think anyone was on the lookout for them, they wouldn't have needed to cover their tracks, would they? So they could have used a legit motor. Anyway, lot of villains work behind the cover of some kind of front business, don't they?'

'True.' Jukebox's mouse clicked on another icon, and lines of data began to stream quickly up the screen. 'Just take a minute and we'll be there.' He sat back, waiting for the computer to complete its search. 'Want a cup of tea or anything, either of you?'

'Not for me, thanks.'

'Nor me,' said Gary. 'You doing mostly this research stuff these days, are you, Jukebox?'

'Yes. Seems to be quite a demand for it. In the old days police information was always a bit iffy, but now they've updated their operating systems, they're really quite efficient. So you can pick up some useful stuff.'

'No problems hacking in?'

'With the police?' Jukebox Jarvis snorted with laughter. 'You gotta be joking. Well, they have a new six-letter password each day ...'

'Funny,' said Truffler. 'We was only talking about that last night.'

'Anyway,' Jukebox went on, 'I've devised a programme that can test out all the available options on that within thirty seconds.'

'Handy.'

'Right. Not that the police are very inventive at the best of times, anyway.

Hardly believe what today's password was
...'

'Go on, amaze us. Not "police" or "secret" this time, was it?'

'No. It was "copper".' They all laughed. 'You know, crime writers may invent policemen who appreciate opera and write poetry, but I'm afraid the real Plods are still pretty primitive in the old imagination stakes.' He moved forward as the fast-moving data on his screen stabilized. 'Ah, we're getting something.' He pointed to the relevant entry. 'There it is—a red Transit—and there's your registration. Owner's name mean anything, me old kipper?'

Truffler leant his long body forward to take a look at the screen. '"R.D. D'Acosta",' he read. 'Oh yes, that means something to me all right.'

'Vehicle's registered to a car spares company. Looks like our friend D'Acosta owns a breaker's yard.'

'That'd figure. Though I think most of what gets broken there'd be bones.' Truffler nodded at the recollection. 'Oh yes, I know him of old. Rod D'Acosta. South London villain. Special subject—GBH.'

'But someone like Rod D'Acosta's never

going to be into art theft, is he?' Gary objected.

'Too right. He couldn't tell a Picasso from a picnic basket. The D'Acosta boys are strictly Rent-A-Muscle.' Truffler Mason rubbed his long chin thoughtfully. 'No, Rod D'Acosta's got to be working for someone else on this job. Now, I wonder who that someone else might be ...?'

Chapter Twenty-Three

Detective Inspector Craig Wilkinson was no fool. He was aware that this was not everyone's opinion. But the fact that he was aware that this was not everyone's opinion, to his mind, proved that he was no fool.

The way he had dismissed Sergeant Hughes's theories about a connection between the late Mr Pargeter and the Mrs Pargeter he had met outside the betting shop had not been evidence of stupidity. It had been calculated. Wilkinson distrusted Hughes. He distrusted his cockiness and impetuous enthusiasm. Every detective at the start of his career assumed that he could change the world and defeat the entire criminal community in a matter of moments. It was important such people learnt that things moved rather more slowly in the Police Force. They had to develop the correct approach to the profession on which they were embarking, an approach which Inspector Wilkinson felt, without false modesty, that he exemplified perfectly.

So poo-pooing Sergeant Hughes's theories had been part of a long-term plan, a plan which would serve two purposes. First, it would put the cocky young man in his place. Second, it would put him off the scent, thus giving Inspector Wilkinson a breathing space in which to pursue his own enquiries. Oh no, the inspector had an agenda all right. The fact that he maintained there to be no connection between the late Mr Pargeter and Mrs Pargeter did not necessarily mean that that was what he believed.

The foyer to Greene's Hotel was impressive, more country house than commercial establishment, but the Inspector was not daunted by it. A good copper, he knew, was never daunted by surroundings. He had conducted too many interviews in lavish surroundings to be fazed by them. And in many cases he had found that lavish surroundings proved to contain thumping crooks.

There was a man in a black jacket and striped trousers behind the antique desk which was presumably the hotel's Reception. He looked distantly familiar, though the inspector couldn't say from where. The man looked up at the visitor's approach.

'Good afternoon, Inspector,' he said. 'Can I help you?'

'Yes, I wonder if you could ...' Suspicion darted in Wilkinson's deepset eyes. 'Just a minute. Why did you call me "Inspector"?'

The hotel manager looked flustered. 'I'm sorry,' he mumbled. 'Our regular inspection from Health and Safety is due today, and I just assumed that you were their representative.'

'Well, I'm not.'

'No, I'm very sorry about the confusion,' the hotel manager, all urbane charm, apologized. 'So what *can* I do for you, sir?'

'I understand you have a Mrs Pargeter staying here ...'

'That is correct, yes.'

'Do you happen to know if she is in the hotel at the moment?'

'Yes, Inspector Wilkinson, she is.'

'Oh well, I'd be very grateful if ...' Once again suspicion surfaced in the Inspector's eyes. 'Just a minute. Why did you call me "Inspector Wilkinson"?'

'Oh, um, well ...' Fluster returned to the hotel manager's manner. 'The thing is, the gentleman I was expecting from Health and Safety was called "Inspector Wilkinson", and I'm afraid I must have still been thinking of that. You know how it is ... once one gets an idea fixed in one's mind ...'

'Yes,' said Wilkinson, not entirely convinced.

'Anyway, you were asking about Mrs Pargeter ...'

'Yes. Could you please ring up to her room—'

'Suite.'

'To her suite, and ask if she would be free to have a word with me?'

'Of course.' The hotel manager reached for an old-fashioned telephone on the desk and started dialling a number.

'You haven't asked me what my name is.'

'What?'

'You don't know who I am. Do you normally announce unidentified visitors to your residents?'

'No, no, of course I don't.' A button was pressed to stop the phone from ringing. 'What name should I say, sir?'

'My name is Inspector Wilkinson.'

'Good heavens!' The hotel manager seemed to have something troubling his throat. But for the fact that there was nothing funny in the situation, Wilkinson could almost have imagined the man was trying to suppress a laugh. 'Well, what a remarkable coincidence. That you and the Health and Safety inspector should both have the same ... I don't know, it's the kind of thing, if you read it in a book, you wouldn't believe it.'

A trembling hand once again dialled the relevant number, and this time got through. 'Ah, Mrs Pargeter. It's Mr Clinton down at the front desk. I have a gentleman who would like to have a word with you.' He seemed to be having some problem with something in his mouth, and started coughing. Through his coughs—which somehow didn't quite sound like coughs he managed to say, 'His name ... is Inspector ... Craig ... Wilkinson ...' The coughing continued as he put the phone down and turned back to the visitor. 'She says ...' he croaked, 'that ... she'll come down to the bar ... straight away ...'

'Oh, fine. Whereabouts is the ...?' But suspicion once again waylaid the Inspector. 'Just a minute. Why did you call me "Inspector *Craig* Wilkinson"? I didn't tell you my first name was Craig.'

'No, no, you didn't ...' Fluster and coughing fought for control of the unfortunate hotel manager. 'No, no, I think, um ... Do you know, you're not going to believe this ...'

'Try me,' said Wilkinson implacably.

'... but the first name of the Inspector who was due from Health and Safety was also Craig.'

There was a silence. Then the inspector shrugged. 'Oh well, that *is* a coincidence. Which way's the bar?'

A trembling finger pointed and he followed its direction. Fortunately he was actually inside the bar and out of earshot before Hedgeclipper Clinton's control finally gave up the unequal struggle.

Chapter Twenty-Four

'Now what will you have to drink? Champagne?' asked Mrs Pargeter, once they were settled into the luxury of the bar.

Wilkinson looked at his watch. 'It's only four o'clock in the afternoon.'

'Yes, I know, but what I like about champagne is that it has no respect for the hour of the day. Come on, surely you'll have something?'

He stroked his moustache dubiously. 'Well, I'm not sure ...'

'Is it the old "no, not while I'm on duty" thing?'

'No, no, it's not that.'

'Do you mean you're *not* on duty?'

'No. Not exactly. I mean, I am, in a manner of speaking on duty. A good copper, you know, is never off duty. Always alert, always looking out for tiny things, for those tell-tale details which don't seem significant at the time, but which later turn out to be relevant.'

'Yes, of course. And often, I find, one's eye is sharper to spot those tiny things after one's had a drink or two.' An almost imperceptible flick of a finger brought the barman gliding to her side. 'Now, you will join me, won't you?'

Wilkinson melted under the violet-blue beam that was focused on him. 'Well, all right, that'd be very nice, thank you.'

'Now, are you happy with champagne?'

'Erm, well ...' He looked awkward. 'I'm really more of a beer man myself.'

'You have beers, don't you, Leon?'

The barman nodded. 'Of course. Which would you like, sir? There's the Narodni Urquel from Czechoslokavia, Mexican Sombrero, Tiger Tail from India, Australian Sheepshearer's Armpit, Japanese Tikkoo, San Felipe from Chile, Ghanaian Lion's Breath or Icelandic Grurttstoffstrottir.' Wilkinson opened his mouth to reply, but wasn't quick enough. 'Then, of course, from America we have Beckweiser, Buck's, Cools, Boston Steam Packet and beers from microbreweries in Monterey, Galveston and New Paltz.'

'Hmm,' said the Inspector. 'You don't by any chance have a pint of English bitter, do you?'

'I could send out for one, sir,' the barman replied.

'Well, if you could, I'd be most grateful.'

'Of course. So, Mrs Pargeter, will it just be a half-bottle of the champagne for you?'

'Oh, no, make it a full one. I'm sure it'll get drunk.' The barman nodded agreement. 'Just so long as I don't, eh?'

She giggled and, while Leon went off to fix their order, turned her full attention on Inspector Wilkinson. 'Now what can I do for you?'

The Inspector lit up a cigarette, before he began. 'Well ...'

She interrupted, 'I would just like to take this opportunity to thank you for all you do.'

'Me? But you don't know what I do.'

'I didn't mean you specifically. I meant you as a representative of the British Police Force. I just wanted to say that you're a wonderful band of men, and I'm sometimes afraid that all your hard work gets a little bit under-appreciated.'

The hotel manager, who was passing through the bar at that moment, seemed suddenly to be afflicted by another bout of coughing.

'That's all I wanted to say,' Mrs Pargeter concluded, 'but it's just something that I don't think gets said often enough.'

'No, well, I would go along with that,' Inspector Wilkinson agreed.

'You belong to a fine body of men, and I can see that you're a fine man yourself. And I think everyone should help the police whenever they possibly can. You do a tough job and, if there's anything a member of the public can do to make that job easier, they should do it. You will certainly have my full cooperation. You can rely on me to assist you in any way at all.'

Inspector Wilkinson glowed visibly at this flattery and preened his moustache. 'That is much appreciated, Mrs Pargeter. Thank you very much.'

Exotic Japanese cocktail nibbles appeared on the table between them. They were quickly joined by a pint of bitter on a silver coaster, a champagne flute and, by the side of the table, an ice bucket with an opened bottle in it.

'Pour away,' said Mrs Pargeter, as Leon was about to offer her some to taste. She raised the twinkling glass to her lips. 'Cheers, Inspector.'

'Down the hatch.' He took a long swallow from his pint.

'Incidentally, calling you "Inspector" does sound horribly formal, doesn't it?'

'Well ...'

'What's your first name?'

'Craig.'

'Well, do you mind if I call you "Craig", Craig?'

Once again the violet-blue beam worked its magic. 'No, Mrs Pargeter. I would be extremely honoured.'

'Good.' She sat back in her chair and took another swallow of champagne. 'This is cosy, isn't it?'

'Yes. Yes, very.' Craig Wilkinson took another long pull at his pint. A peaceable silence descended between them.

It was Mrs Pargeter who at last broke it. 'Well...' she began tentatively, 'did I gather there was something you wanted to ask me?'

'Yes. Of course.' Wilkinson shook himself out of his reverie. 'Yes, I wished to make some enquiries about your late husband ...'

'Fine. About what in particular?'

'Well, Mrs Pargeter, it was kind of in relation to his business dealings ...'

'I'll tell you anything I can, Craig ...' He simpered at the use of his first name. She chuckled apologetically. 'But I'm afraid there's a lot I just don't know. My husband and I belonged to the generation when men didn't bring their work home with them. If ever I asked anything about his business affairs, he'd say, "Don't you worry your pretty little head about that, Melita my love," and that was it. I know today's young independent feminists wouldn't approve of that kind of attitude, but I must say I always found it very comforting.'

'Yes, yes, I can see that ...' The Inspector shifted in his chair and flicked a column of ash into the ashtray. He wasn't finding it easy to get to the point that concerned him. 'Not a very common name, Pargeter, is it?'

'No,' she agreed. 'I think it's a lovely name, though. I was so pleased to take it on when we got married—another thing I dare say the feminist brigade would disapprove of.'

'Quite probably, yes.' Wilkinson found it difficult to stop himself from smiling. There was something about this plump, self-assured, comfortable woman that engendered smiles.

'A "pargeter" was actually a plasterer,' she went on. 'Rather upmarket one, though. Did all that fancy plasterwork on the front of Tudor buildings.'

'Really? That's fascinating.'

'It is, isn't it?' Peace re-descended between them. Again it was Mrs Pargeter who moved the conversation on. 'So what was it you wanted to ask about my husband's business affairs, Craig?'

'Well, Mrs Pargeter ...' He now found himself acutely embarrassed. In the atmosphere that had developed between them, his question seemed incongruous. He looked down at his large shoes as he pressed on. 'I just wondered if you'd ever heard any suggestion that some of your late husband's business dealings were in any way ... criminal?'

She did not respond immediately, and Wilkinson looked up, expecting to read affront in her face. But instead what greeted him was helpless, though silent, laughter. Tears glistened over the violet-blue eyes.

'Criminal?' she finally managed to gasp. 'Criminal? My husband—involved in something criminal? Oh, I wish he was in this room to hear you say that.'

'Why?'

'Well, if you'd ever known him, you'd realize that ...' Again she struggled for words. 'He'd be so offended by the suggestion. My husband was the most strait-laced and correct man I think I've ever met. He had a punctilious—almost an obsessive—respect for the law. Particularly the British legal system. "Finest in the world," he'd always say. "Absolute finest in the entire universe!" And the idea of him being involved in anything even mildly shady ...' She roared with laughter. 'I'm sorry. Your question was just so unexpected. And in relation to my husband, so hysterically funny. I mean, I loved him dearly, but I have to say, when it came to moral issues, he was a bit of an old fuddy-duddy. I mean, if he found a 10p coin on the pavement, he'd go to the police station to hand it in. That's the kind of man he was. And the idea that he might have had criminal connections ...' Once again she was incapacitated by peals of laughter.

It was more than an hour later that Detective Inspector Craig Wilkinson left Greene's Hotel. A couple more pints of English bitter had been sent out for, and

Mrs Pargeter had got through the bulk of her bottle of champagne. The atmosphere between them had been very relaxed.

Wilkinson felt positively boyish as he hailed a cab to take him to his flat. His instinct had been vindicated. He'd been right once again. And he'd take enormous pleasure in telling that to Sergeant Hughes.

A good copper, as the Inspector so often said, was never off duty. Always alert, always looking out for tiny things, for those tell-tale details which don't seem significant at the time, but which later turn out to have enormous relevance.

And Mrs Pargeter had said something to him which, in retrospect, he recognized to have mind-blowingly enormous relevance. Maybe Craig Wilkinson was about to make his mark, after all.

Chapter Twenty-Five

It had always been Mrs Pargeter's view that business and pleasure could—and indeed should—be mixed. If a meeting could be accompanied by a little refreshment, so much the better. If it could be accompanied by a lavish dinner, expertly devised by the award-winning chef of Greene's Hotel, better still.

So it was that that evening found her sitting at her favourite table in the restaurant, in the company of Hedgeclipper Clinton and the magnificent Hamish Ramon Henriques. No one would ever have known, from her graceful manner, that Mrs Pargeter had, only a few hours before, consumed a whole bottle of champagne.

She had reported her conversation with Inspector Wilkinson to the travel agent, though her narrative had been constantly interrupted by recollections and ribaldry from Hedgeclipper. HRH knew all about the Inspector and was appropriately amused by their accounts. 'I don't think the stick exists anywhere in the world that that guy isn't capable of getting the wrong end of.'

'Well, at the end of our conversation he certainly seemed convinced that I had nothing to do with my late husband.'

'That's absolutely typical. True to form, eh, Hedgeclipper?'

'You bet. Faced with the widow of one

of the biggest criminal masterminds in the history of—'

'I *beg* your pardon?' asked Mrs Pargeter icily.

'Ah, well, I, er ... Sorry,' the hotel manager floundered.

HRH interceded fluently, 'I think Mr Clinton was just endorsing my view that Inspector Wilkinson will always be guaranteed to get the wrong end of the stick. Isn't that right?'

'Yes. Yes. Exactly.'

The chilling glare of the violet-blue eyes remained on Hedgeclipper's face for a second longer, before Mrs Pargeter relaxed, sat back and took another sip of champagne. But there was a trace of anxiety in her voice when she asked, 'Are you sure you're right, though? You don't think it's possible that Inspector Wilkinson was playing an elaborate double bluff?'

'Rest assured, my dear Mrs Pargeter,' said HRH, 'you need have no worries on that score. Craggy Wilkinson is incapable of a double bluff. He's only just capable of a single bluff.'

'And even then, not an elaborate one,' added Hedgeclipper Clinton.

'Oh, good, I'm glad to hear it.'

Hamish Ramon Henriques provided even more reassurance. 'Don't worry about a thing. Jukebox Jarvis'll keep an eye on what's happening on the police computer. If Wilkinson has any genuine suspicions, we'll know about them before the other people in his office do.'

'Thanks. That's really nice to know.'

Mrs Pargeter sat back in her chair, the iciness of a few moments before completely forgotten. She munched contentedly on her starter, a fantasy of quails' eggs and langoustines, and watched as the travel agent produced a sheaf of neatly typed and stapled pages. It was very comforting, she found, to know she was working with professionals.

'I've been through Palings Price's list,' said HRH, 'of all the stuff he reckons was in Chastaigne Varleigh, and sorted out personnel to do the actual returning of all the paintings.'

'May I have a look?' asked Hedgeclipper.

'Of course.'

The hotel manager ran a practised eye down the lines of text, as Mrs Pargeter said, 'Well, I just hope it hasn't raised any problems for you, HRH ...'

'None at all,' he replied, all urbanity.

'When a philanthropist like your husband passes on, he leaves many people who are only too happy to take on some small task to express their gratitude to him.'

Mrs Pargeter allowed the recurrent compliment a little misty-eyed nod.

Hedgeclipper Clinton tapped the sheet in front of him. 'I didn't know old Vanishing Vernon was still around, HRH.'

'Certainly.' He turned to Mrs Pargeter. 'I should explain that we're referring to one of your late husband's most trusted aides.'

'Oh.' She smiled vaguely. The name meant nothing to her. Throughout their marriage she had ensured that the names of most of her husband's associates meant nothing to her (which was why it was so easy to maintain an expression of genuine innocence in the face of enquiries from people like Inspector Wilkinson). 'And why,' she asked, 'was he called Vanishing Vernon? Bit of a Houdini, was he? Could make himself disappear?'

Hedgeclipper Clinton chuckled. 'No, it wasn't himself he made disappear—it was other people.'

'Oh.'

She would not have pursued the matter

further, but HRH felt some gloss was required. 'Though, I should hasten to point out, Mrs Pargeter, Vanishing Vernon never used any violence.'

'Well,' Hedgeclipper conceded, 'not more than was absolutely necessary.'

'No. He just tended to ... drive inconvenient people away in his car.'

Mrs Pargeter smiled easily. 'That sounds quite civilized.'

'Yes,' HRH agreed, slightly less easily.

'Mind you,' said Hedgeclipper, 'he did drive them away in the boot rather than the back seat.'

'But I must again stress, Mrs Pargeter—without violence. Inconvenient people would just tend to ... wake up feeling very sleepy ... isn't that right, Hedgeclipper?'

'Yes ... Sleepy—and 300 miles from where they last remembered being.'

'Ah.' Again Mrs Pargeter felt disinclined to enquire further.

The hotel manager shook his head in fond recollection. 'Anyway, I'm surprised to hear old Vanishing's still around. Not in the business any more, is he, HRH?'

Affront at this suggestion trembled the travel agent's splendid growth of whiskers. 'Good heavens, no. His current activities are one-hundred per cent legitimate.'

'So what does he do now then?' asked Mrs Pargeter with an ingenuous smile.

'He organizes car boot sales.'

Outside a very suburban semi in North London the next morning was parked an oldish VW camper van, its back windows nearly obscured by the quantities of holiday paraphernalia packed inside. In the passenger seat sat VVO. He looked at his scruffiest, the archetype of the misunderstood genius. The cliché beret sat defiantly on his head.

He watched as his wife Deirdre, neat in crisp fondant-green shirt and shorts, locked the front door and clacked on white high heels down the garden path. She got in the driver's side of the camper van, started the engine and looked fondly across at her husband.

VVO grinned back in sheepish excitement. 'I can't believe I'm really being allowed to do this, Deirdre—go off on my own hazardous mission.'

She patted his thigh. 'Well, you are, Reg Winthrop. Mrs Pargeter trusts you, so don't you dare screw up.'

'I won't, love. Because I've never been

put to the test, nobody knows just how cool I can be in a crisis.'

'Hmm ...' Deirdre looked her husband up and down, appraisingly. 'And remember what HRH said—don't do anything that's going to draw attention to yourself.'

'No,' he agreed, evading her glance. But when he looked back, her eye was still beadily fixed on his beret. After only a nanosecond of hesitation, he removed it. 'Right you are, love.'

Deirdre Winthrop, secure in the complete control she had over her husband, put the camper van in gear, and they set off towards Dover.

Caught up in their mutual excitement, they did not notice that an unobtrusive car started up soon after them and stayed, only two or three vehicles behind, all the way to the South Coast. And, even if they had noticed it, because they'd never met him, they wouldn't have known that it was being driven by Sergeant Hughes.

Chapter Twenty-Six

The trilling of the bedside telephone insinuated itself into Mrs Pargeter's morning dream of some sylvan picnic with her late husband. Slowly she opened her eyes, greeting this day, like every other, with enormous confidence and the knowledge that things were bound to go well for her. She felt serenely rested. The lavish dinner of the night before—and the full bottle of champagne before it—had left her with nothing so vulgar as a hangover, merely a delicious sense of having been pampered, and having deserved it.

She looked across to the photograph on the bedside table. The suited image of her late husband smiled gravely back at her. 'Morning, love,' she said, as she did every morning. 'I was only talking about you yesterday. Saying what an admirer of the British legal system you were. And what a punctilious old fuddy-duddy you were when it came to moral issues.'

Next she consulted her watch. Nearly half past nine. Very satisfactory.

The telephone trilled on. She reached across and answered it. 'Hello?'

'It's me,' a familiar voice intoned.

'Truffler, how good to hear you.'

'Just ringing to say we've found out where the paintings are.'

'Brilliant. I knew you would. Going to have any problems getting them out?'

Truffler Mason, mobile phone pressed to his cheek, looked across at the red Transit van. There was no question he'd found the right one. The number plate tallied with what had appeared on Jukebox Jarvis's computer screen. It was Rod D'Acosta's vehicle all right.

But Truffler was looking at it through the padlocked gates of a car breaker's yard. This was a thickly walled lot, with barbed-wire defences running round the top of the wall. The area was decorated with a large number of signs bearing such deterrent legends as 'ELECTRONIC ALARMS IN OPERATION' and 'GUARD DOGS PATROL THESE PREMISES'.

'Yes,' said Truffler Mason, in reply to Mrs Pargeter's question. 'Maybe a few problems.'

Chapter Twenty-Seven

A queue of lorries shunted slowly through the Customs shed at Dover. Second in line was a venerable VW camper van. In its passenger seat Deirdre Winthrop was a little agitated. Her husband, now the driver, also looked tense. In defiance of Deirdre, he had put his beret back on again.

His wife looked anxiously out of the window. 'I'm sure we shouldn't have got into this queue, Reg. We should have gone straight on to the ferry. You don't have to stop for Customs these days unless they ask you to. And certainly not on the English side.'

'Give me the benefit of the doubt, please, dear,' said her husband manfully. 'I do know what I'm doing.'

'But I don't think—'

VVO patronized her with a confident smile. 'Nobody knows just how cool I can be in a crisis.'

'There'd be no crisis if you hadn't

stuck your neck out by ...' Her words trickled away as she realized that the lorry ahead had trundled off. They were now at the head of the queue. VVO eased the camper van forward till the breezy face of a Customs Officer appeared framed in the driver's side window.

The Customs Officer, full of *entente cordiale* and *bonhomie,* responded to VVO's beret. *'Bonjour monsieur.'*

'Actuellement,' said the artist, *'nous sommes English.'*

'Ah. *Vraiment?'*

'Yes. *Vraiment.'*

'Righty-ho.'The Customs Officer grinned. 'Anything I should know about in this camper then?'

VVO shook his head. 'Nothing of great importance. A few paintings in the back, that's all.'

People who have been married for a long time can feel the subtext of looks which are invisible to outsiders. VVO felt the heat of Deirdre's invisible fury, and she felt the infuriating flabbiness of his 'I know what I'm doing' glance.'

'Paintings?' the Customs Officer echoed. 'Well, maybe I should have a look at those. Depending on what they are, they might need export licences or be liable for duty.'

While Deirdre seethed imperceptibly beside him, the painter got out of the camper. 'Of course.' He led the Customs Officer round the back and opened the double doors. He lifted the covering rugs to reveal his paintings. 'There they are.' It was impossible for VVO to keep the pride out of his voice.

The Officer looked at the canvases. Clearly dealing with a lot of French people had not been without effect. He let out one of those peculiarly Gallic laughs which begins with a 'poof' sound. 'Oh,' he chuckled, as he turned away from the van, 'sorry to have troubled you. No, there's certainly nothing to pay on that lot.'

VVO's kneejerk reaction was entirely predictable. 'What do you mean?' he spluttered.

'Well,' replied the Customs Officer, still chuckling. 'You only have to pay duty on things of value.'

From the front seat of the camper, Deirdre Winthrop was craning round, desperately trying to catch her husband's eye and deflect him from the kamikaze course on which she knew him to be embarked.

'Are you saying these paintings don't have any value?' VVO seethed.

'That is exactly right.' The Customs Officer let out a self-congratulatory giggle as he came up with a *bon mot*. 'I mean, I may not know much about art, but I know what I don't like.'

The painter was now beside himself with fury. He had been hit where it really hurt—in his art. 'How dare you!' he screamed. 'You philistine! Those paintings are brilliant—they're worth any sum you care to mention!'

'Oh really?' A colder, more calculating look came into the Customs Officer's eyes. He moved back towards the camper. 'Well, maybe I'd better have a closer look at them then ...'

As the Officer leant in towards the paintings, over his bent back Deirdre Winthrop finally caught her husband's eye. The look she beamed at him on this occasion was not a private intramarital one. If looks could kill, hers should have left a large, messy exit-wound somewhere round the back of VVO's head. With bowed shoulders, the artist meekly returned to the driver's seat. A silence that felt even longer than it was elapsed.

Eventually, the Customs Officer closed the doors and took his time walking back to the front of the van. There was a tense silence, then he said, 'No, no problem with any of that lot.'

'You mean we can go?' asked Deirdre, scarcely able to believe their luck.

'Yes, sure. You can—' He was interrupted by a tone from the radio telephone he had clipped to his belt. 'Excuse me a moment. Hello?' he said into the phone. 'Who? Sergeant Hughes? No, I don't know who you are ...'

'Drive off,' Deirdre Winthrop hissed at her husband.

'What?'

'Drive *off!*'

'Oh, really?' said the Customs Officer, with a new significance in his tone. 'Yes, I will.' His eyes narrowed as he looked back at the Winthrops. 'If you'd be so kind as to wait a little longer, there are just a couple of things I'd like to check ...'

'Oh, *Reg!*' Deirdre murmured in anguish.

Chapter Twenty-Eight

Inspector Wilkinson sat at his desk, running his tongue along his top lip. His moustache, he decided, was nearly long enough to chew. What should he do—trim it that evening when he got home, or let it grow until he'd got something that was really worth chewing? God, life was difficult. Decisions, decisions. It was no fun being a senior detective.

His telephone rang. He resented the intrusion. He'd rather it had rung *after* he'd made the decision about whether or not to trim his moustache.

He deliberately let the phone ring on while he lit another cigarette, then answered it. 'Hello? Wilkinson.'

'It's Sergeant Hughes, sir.'

'Oh yes? I thought it was your day off.'

'It is, sir. I'm in Dover.'

'Nipping over the Channel on a quick booze cruise, are you?'

'No, sir. I'm working.'

186

Wilkinson was appalled. 'On your day off?' That kind of thing hadn't happened in the Inspector's young day.

'Yes, sir. I've been following up a lead on the art thefts.'

'Hughes, I have told you before. *I* am in charge of this case. In our business, if you have lots of different people running off in all directions without telling anyone ... well, anarchy ensues.'

'I know, sir, but—'

'Everyone should know their place. I mean, what would have happened to this great country of ours throughout its history if people hadn't done what they were told? A good copper obeys orders. All the great men of our history have obeyed orders. Alfred the Great, Drake, Nelson—'

'Actually, Nelson didn't.'

'What?'

'Nelson was quite famous for not obeying orders, sir. In the summer of 1799, he was ordered to take his ships to Minorca, but he thought the French threat would be towards Naples, so he disobeyed. And then, of course, at the Battle of Copenhagen in 1801, he famously raised the telescope to his blind eye and said, "I really do not see the signal", and then—'

'All right, Hughes,' Wilkinson interrupted testily, *'all right!* There's another
thing you should remember if you're
hoping to get anywhere in the Police
Force.'

'And what's that, sir?'

'Nobody likes a smart-arse.' Wilkinson
harrumphed, removed his cigarette to
offload its accumulation of ash, and ran
the tip of his tongue along the line of his
moustache.

'But, sir, I've been following a lead, and
it's led somewhere!'

'Well, that's a novelty in this business,'
said the Inspector sarcastically. 'What lead
is this, Hughes?'

'You know I've been going back through
the old files connected with the art thefts
...'

'I thought I told you to stop doing
that.'

Sergeant Hughes ignored the reprimand
and went on, 'Well, I came across this
reference to a top-level informant ...'

'Are you talking about the one who
called himself "Posey Narker"?'

'Yes, sir.'

Inspector Wilkinson let out a world-
weary sigh. 'Sergeant, Posey Narker has

long since gone to ground. There's been nothing heard from him since the death of the late Mr Pargeter.'

'I know that, sir, but I still thought it might be worth ringing his number.'

'Why?'

'Just on the off chance.'

'*Just on the off chance?*' The repetition dripped with scorn. 'Hughes, a good copper doesn't do anything just on the off chance. A good copper works things out in detail, he plans, he uses his intellect. Good heavens, where do you think the Met would be if all our detectives went around doing things just on the off chance? Can you name a single occasion on which anyone got a result from doing something just on the off chance?'

'Yes, sir.'

'When?'

'I got a result this morning, sir, just on the off chance.' Hughes couldn't keep the crowing note out of his voice.

'Oh, did you?'

'As I said, I rang the number for Posey Narker just on the off chance, and early this morning I had a call back. Untraceable, mobile number he was calling from, but he gave me some very useful information.'

'Really, Hughes?' Inspector Wilkinson spoke as if to an overtired five-year-old. 'Well, you follow up on that lead when you're next on duty, eh? For today, this is what I want you to do: you go straight back home, have a nice relaxing afternoon, watch some sport on the telly perhaps ... and come in tomorrow morning ready for a proper—and authorized—day's work.'

'I'm sorry, sir, but I'm afraid I can't leave Dover.'

'Why not?'

'Because I've found three of the missing paintings, sir.'

'WHAT!!!?'

Chapter Twenty-Nine

'Interview with Mr Reginald Winthrop conducted at Dover Police Station on 17 September. Also present Detective Inspector Craig Wilkinson, Detective Sergeant Hercule Hughes ... Funny, I didn't know you were called Hercule.'

The Sergeant blushed. 'My mother was a great fan of Agatha Christie, sir.'

'And saw you becoming a great detective too, eh?'

'I'm not sure that—'

'A great detective is one who is prepared to put in a lot of hard slog—and also one who obeys orders, Hughes. Oh, it's fine for your amateur Belgians with fatuous curly moustaches to keep going off at tangents and "following their instincts", "listening to the little grey cells", but a good copper does what he's told and when he's—'

'Sir,' Sergeant Hughes whispered, 'this is all going on tape.'

'Yes, yes, of course it is. Mmm.' Wilkinson cleared his throat. 'Interview commenced at 3.17 p.m.'

The Inspector gazed into space, apparently not seeing the nervous man in a beret who sat on the other side of the table. The silence lengthened, until Sergeant Hughes made a pointed cough.

'Hmm?' Wilkinson seemed to have difficulty dragging himself back from his reverie. In fact, it had been prompted by something he himself had said. 'Fatuous curly moustaches'. Maybe on him that kind of thing wouldn't look fatuous.

If he didn't trim his for months and trained it and covered it with pomade ... whatever pomade might be—apple juice, he wondered ... anyway, if he did all that, the effect might suit him rather well. And people would certainly remember what he looked like. Perhaps it was through his physical appearance that Craig Wilkinson could make his mark ...?

'Don't you think we should get on with the interview?' Hughes prompted again.

'What? Oh yes.' Wilkinson fixed the painter with a beady eye. VVO looked away shiftily. 'Mr Winthrop, we have talked at length to your wife, who maintains that she knew nothing about the contents of the van, other than the holiday luggage and other equipment whose packing she supervised. She says she knew there were three of your paintings in the back, and assumed that you had packed them with a view to trying to open up new markets for their sale on the continent. She denies knowing that there were expensive Old Masters hidden behind your artwork. And ...' the Inspector concluded, 'I am inclined to believe her. For that reason, she has been released from our custody.'

'Yes, I know that,' said VVO grumpily.

'I know you know that, but I am merely reiterating it so that all information that might be required is recorded on the tape. Now, Mr Winthrop, although I am convinced of your wife's innocence, I have yet to be in the same happy state with regard to your own involvement. I find it very hard to believe that you were unaware of what you were carrying in that camper van.'

'Well, I was. I've told you. Why don't you listen?'

'I do listen, Mr Winthrop, but I'm afraid what I hear does not leave me any more convinced. Whoever framed those pictures of yours must've known that the other paintings were fixed behind them. Of course, we will be checking the frames for fingerprints ...'

VVO hadn't considered that possibility. It really could screw things up; he had no doubt his fingerprints were all over everything. Still, they hadn't checked them yet. If he kept on protesting his innocence, maybe they could be persuaded to believe him. It was a long shot, he knew, but he had to play for time. Once Truffler Mason and the others heard what had happened, he was sure they could start some kind of damage limitation operation. His own stupidity, the arrogant assumption that he could sail so close to the wind and get away with it, had landed him in this pickle, and now it was up to him to ensure that he didn't make the situation any worse. The main thing, he knew, was not to mention any names of other people involved.

VVO brought himself back to the present. Inspector Wilkinson was speaking again. 'Maybe you have some explanation of how the paintings got to be there, Mr Winthrop ...? If you do, I'd be fascinated to hear it.'

'I bought them like that,' he replied brazenly. 'I usually buy canvases ready prepared, and those three must've had the stolen paintings hidden in them before they came into my possession.'

'I see,' said the Inspector, in a way that suggested he didn't see at all. 'Well, of course we can check with your supplier. Was it the place you usually use?'

'Yes.'

'Could we have the name, please?'

VVO gave it, thinking that when—if ever—he got out of his current mess, there was one highly respectable artists' materials supplier he wouldn't be able to use again. Still, it was all taking time, all part of his delaying tactics.

'Incidentally,' the Sergeant suddenly interposed, You described them as "stolen" paintings, Mr Winthrop. Neither of us said they were stolen. How did you know?'

The older detective looked daggers at his subordinate. 'The very question *I* had been about to ask, Hughes—if you'd given me time.'

'Sorry, sir.'

Wilkinson stared again into the artist's eyes. VVO again turned away. 'So, Mr Winthrop, how did you know they were stolen?'

Bluster seemed to be the appropriate response. 'Simple, old-fashioned common sense, Inspector! How many Old Masters do you know of which aren't either in museums or private ownership? And on the rare occasions they are moved around, it's in security vans, not stuffed down the back of other paintings. Of course they were stolen!'

'You may have a point,' Wilkinson conceded.

Sergeant Hughes leant forward. 'Does the name "Pargeter" mean anything to you, Mr Winthrop?'

'Will you please not interrupt, Hughes!' the Inspector snapped. 'I am the senior officer present. I should dictate the direction this interview takes.'

'I'm sorry, sir. I just thought, possibly catching him off guard with a sudden question might—'

'You've watched too many cop shows, Sergeant.' Wilkinson turned to VVO with a polite smile. 'I'm so sorry.'

'No problem.'

'Right,' the Inspector went on. 'Does the name "Pargeter" mean anything to you, Mr Winthrop?'

'As in "Mrs Pargeter",' Sergeant Hughes added eagerly.

'No, Hughes, not as in "Mrs Pargeter". As in "Mr Pargeter", Mr Winthrop?'

'No.'

'If I'd said "Mrs Pargeter", would that have meant any more?'

'No.'

'What about the name "Bennie Logan"? Does that mean anything to you?'

'No.'

'Fritzi the Finger?'

'No.'

Hmm, thought Inspector Wilkinson ruefully, this is going to take a long time.

VVO, though with rather more glee, had exactly the same thought.

Wilkinson ran a finger along the line of his moustache. Maybe he should trim it, after all.

Chapter Thirty

Mrs Pargeter put the newspaper down ruefully. She'd read the report, and it had brought home to her the extent of her short-sightedness. Someone called Reginald Winthrop had been arrested for trying to smuggle stolen paintings out of the country. 'Well, I'm sorry,' was all she could find to say.

'It wasn't your fault, Mrs Pargeter,' said Hamish Ramon Henriques gallantly.

'No, of course it wasn't,' the loyal Truffler Mason agreed.

'Yes, it was.' She looked around HRH's office, the expression on her face as near as it ever got to gloomy. Through the half-open door, she could see neatly uniformed Sharons and Laurens and Karens busy about their business. Mrs Pargeter sighed.

'I shouldn't have given VVO the job. I was guilty of sentimentality.'

HRH shrugged. 'Well ...'

She continued her self-recrimination. 'My husband wouldn't have made that mistake.'

'Perhaps not.'

'"In dealings with employees," he always said, "be always compassionate, but never indulgent!" And of course, as ever, he was right. Don't worry, I'll learn,' said Mrs Pargeter through gritted teeth.

'Of course you will,' the travel agent reassured.

'I've spoken to Deirdre Winthrop. I thought she'd be absolutely devastated, but in fact she's too angry for that. "Serve Reg bloody well right!" were her precise words. "That'll teach him to try and play the hero. What did he imagine—that his flirting with danger was going to turn me on? He should know by now, after twenty-four years of marriage, the only thing that turns me on is a nice quiet life." Of course she didn't know anything about the paintings in the back of the van.'

'No,' said Truffler. 'And I gather VVO's taking the whole blame himself. Apparently he's clamming up on the police, refusing to give the names of anyone else involved, claiming he was working alone.'

'Which is good news for us,' HRH observed.

Mrs Pargeter did not comment on this assertion, but, shaking her head again at her own lack of judgement, went on, 'He was really asking for trouble, volunteering to go through Customs this side of the Channel. I suppose, like Deirdre said, he got some kind of kick out of it—same as a kid gets playing "chicken" on a railway line.'

'I'm sure that was it, Mrs P,' Truffler agreed. 'You often find that with inexperienced villains—first time they're allowed to do something on their own, it kind of goes to their heads, they get really excited and well out of order—' Catching a frosty beam from the violet-blue eyes, he concluded lamely, 'or so I've heard.'

Mrs Pargeter sighed. 'Anyway, what's done is done. Let's hope VVO continues to be uncommunicative.'

'He will, don't worry,' said Hamish Ramon Henriques. 'Having screwed up the actual job, there's no way he's going to screw up his behaviour while under arrest as well.'

'Hope you're right. In the meantime,' Mrs Pargeter continued pragmatically, 'I've organized legal representation for him.'

'Who've you got?'

'Arnold Justiman.'

Hamish Ramon Henriques and Truffler Mason nodded approval. Arnold Justiman's legal skills were without parallel. It was said that he could have organized a driving licence for Blind Pew, and got the charges against Jack the Ripper reduced to fines for overdue library books. 'Nothing but the best,' said HRH.

'No,' Mrs Pargeter agreed. 'My late husband let Arnold deal with all his legal affairs.'

'And very well he did it too,' said Truffler. 'But for Arnold, you'd have seen even less of your husband than you did, wouldn't you?'

Another mild frost settled over Mrs Pargeter's expression. 'I'm sorry? I don't know what you mean, Truffler.'

'No. No, of course not.' He moved hastily on to distance himself from the moment of embarrassment. 'What's odd about the whole business is who was in charge of the investigation.'

'Eh?'

'Jukebox Jarvis has done the usual checks in the police computers as to what happened down in Dover, and it turns out VVO was interviewed by none other than our old friend, Craggy Wilkinson.'

'Really?' This was a shock to Mrs Pargeter. After the reassurances given over the dinner at Greene's Hotel, she had rather dismissed the Inspector from her thoughts. 'Do you think we've got him wrong? Do you think he's actually shrewder than his track record suggests?'

'You'd think he'd have to be,' HRH replied, 'by the law of averages. But I still don't see him working something like this out on his own.'

'He didn't do it on his own,' said Truffler. 'He's got a new detective sergeant working with him. Keen, cocky young lad, I gather, glories in the name of Hercule Hughes. I reckon he's the one behind VVO's arrest.'

'Oh dear,' said Mrs Pargeter.

'Nothing to worry about, Mrs P. We'll just keep an eye on the youngster, that's all. Craggy Wilkinson on his own offers no danger. Craggy Wilkinson with an intelligent young sidekick could prove to be more of a challenge.' Truffler Mason gave a mournful grin. 'But don't give it another thought. Forewarned is forearmed. We've got it covered.'

'Oh, that is nice to know.'

'Yes.' Truffler stroked his chin. 'What we must try and work out, though, is what effect VVO's little disaster is going to have on the people who got away with the rest of the paintings.'

'How do you mean?'

'Well ...' Truffler pointed to the newspaper report. 'There's no way now they don't know that someone else is interested.'

'And you're afraid this may make them speed up their plans and start selling off the goods?'

'It's a possibility.'

As he spoke, Truffler Mason nodded gloomily. So did Hamish Ramon Henriques. To her annoyance, Mrs Pargeter found herself giving a gloomy nod too.

Truffler shook his huge head to jolt himself out of the communal despondency. 'I think I'd better go and check it out,' he said.

The Alsatian lying by the padlocked gates of the breaker's yard snored evenly. From the corner of his slack mouth dripped bloody juices from the drugged meat he had so eagerly wolfed down.

In the car parked inside the yard facing the gates, two men, heavies called Ray and Phil, also snored in rhythmic counterpoint. On the dashboard in front of them stood the open thermos flask which had contained their drugged coffee, and the two plastic cups they had drunk it from. In sleep, the craggy lines of the men's battered faces had been ironed out to give them a baby-like, almost cherubic, innocence. Between them were propped up a shotgun and a baseball bat, and against these they leant in touching tranquillity. In the mouth of one of the villains was lodged an infantile thumb.

Truffler Mason's picklocks sorted out the red Transit van's keyhole as easily as they had the padlocks on the back gate of the yard. With a quick look around the floodlit tangle of dead cars to check he was unobserved, Truffler slipped his tall body into the back of the Transit.

Once inside, he produced a pencil torch from his pocket and ran it quickly over the van's contents. The frames were wrapped in rugs for protection, but he could easily move these aside to check which paintings were there. It didn't take long to match the inventory on Palings Price's list. So far none of the art works taken from Chastaigne Varleigh had been moved on. The hoard was intact.

There was a clattering of the main gate outside. Truffler froze, switched off his pencil torch and eased forward over the partition into the driver's cab to see what was going on. Outlined in the open gateway of the yard, backlit by spotlights, stood two burly figures. He had no difficulty in recognizing Rod D'Acosta and the other heavy who had taken the paintings from Chastaigne Varleigh. One carried a baseball bat, the other a pickaxe handle.

Rod dropped to one knee to check on the Alsatian, and rose in fury when he saw the dog's condition. He then pointed angrily to the parked car, and the two men moved towards it.

Seeing the state of the two guards, Rod and his henchman immediately started banging on the car roof with baseball bat and pickaxe handle. The cherubic peace of the heavies called Ray and Phil was rudely shattered.

But by the time the four villains had reached the red Transit van, its doors were once again firmly locked. Truffler Mason had slipped away through the jumbled wreckage of old cars, and melted into the night.

Chapter Thirty-one

'We need to talk to Veronica Chastaigne,' Sergeant Hughes announced.

'Now just a minute, just a minute,' said his boss. 'I'm the one who decides who we need to talk to.'

'All right, you make the decision, but the fact remains that we need to speak to Veronica Chastaigne.'

'On what grounds? She hasn't done anything wrong. We can't charge her with anything.'

'We don't need to talk to her as a suspect. We need to talk to her as a witness. Come on, she's lived all those years at Chastaigne Varleigh. There's no way that she was unaware of what there was up in the Long Gallery.'

'We have no proof that there was anything there shouldn't have been up in the Long Gallery.'

'Oh, for God's sake!'

Inspector Wilkinson's moustache (which he had, incidentally, decided to let grow) bristled with affront. 'What did you say, Hughes?'

The Sergeant looked subdued. 'Sorry, sir.'

'I should think so.'

The Sergeant looked less subdued. 'What I meant to say was: "Oh, for God's sake, *sir!*"'

Wilkinson stared narrowly at his colleague. 'There's a very disrespectful tone creeping into your voice, Hughes, and I don't like it. Never forget that I am your senior officer.'

'I don't get much chance to forget it, do I ... sir?' The worm, which had always shown a propensity for at least looking over its shoulder, was certainly turning now. 'I thought, when I joined the Police Force, that it was an organization in which people worked together.'

The Inspector removed his habitual cigarette to draw in a sharp breath through pursed lips. 'I don't know where you got that idea from.'

'Listen, I was the one who got on to

Posey Narker. I was the one who followed Reginald Winthrop. I suspected that he was carrying the stolen paintings and had him detained at Dover. And then what did I do? I shared my findings with you. And I just wish you'd occasionally repay the compliment.'

Wilkinson shook his head knowingly. 'A good copper, Hughes, is not in the business of repaying compliments. He's in the business of frustrating criminals, and he does that by relying on his experience.'

'But, sir—'

'You don't have any experience, Hughes, so I'm afraid it'll be some time yet before you can be regarded as a good copper.'

Sergeant Hughes slumped in his chair, deflated by the hopelessness of his frustration. Inspector Wilkinson sat at his desk, smiling complacently, puffing on his cigarette and occasionally stroking his slowly burgeoning moustache.

'You know,' he announced after a long silence, 'we need to talk to Veronica Chastaigne.'

Gary's limousine insinuated itself smoothly through the anonymous suburban streets of North London. In the back, between the brown suits of Truffler Mason and Hamish Ramon Henriques, Mrs Pargeter, resplendent in silk print, sat like the filling of a particularly exotic sandwich.

She reached out and gave Truffler's huge hand a maternal pat. 'I hope you weren't taking unnecessary risks.'

'Nah.' A rueful laugh shook his massive frame and he rubbed his chin. 'I was all right, but there was four of them. Rod and three heavies. It's not going to be that easy to get the stuff out.'

'The simplest thing would be just to give the police a tip-off, you know,' HRH suggested.

But Mrs Pargeter quickly quashed that idea. 'No. I gave Veronica Chastaigne my word I'd get those paintings back to their rightful owners.'

The travel agent instantly accepted the logic of her words. 'Yes, of course. I understand completely, Mrs Pargeter.'

Gary's voice filtered through from the front of the car. 'It's a tricky one. We could really do with Mr Pargeter around right now. He'd see the way through this, no problem. One of the great planning brains of all time, he'd got.'

'Exactly, Gary,' said Mrs Pargeter, as

the limousine slowed to a halt in front of the anonymous terraced house. 'Which is the very reason why we're going to see Jukebox. We can still take advantage of my husband's planning brain, you know ...'

With his spaghetti junction of computer equipment and his four guests, there was very little space in Jukebox Jarvis's front room, but by the odd click of the mouse and the odd tap at the keyboard he steered himself deftly through the data on his screen. He fed in the complex demands of the current problem, and rattled through the proffered options until he found exactly what he wanted.

'Chelmsford!' Jukebox Jarvis pronounced triumphantly. His eyes sparkled through the thick glasses.

A communal smile of fulfilled recollection settled on the faces of the three men who watched him. 'Yeah.' An impressed Truffler Mason nodded. 'Chelmsford, of course.'

Gary shook his head in admiration. 'Brilliant. Lot of clever driving needed for Chelmsford, if I remember right.'

HRH grinned with satisfaction. 'And

some intriguing specialized work required on the vehicles.'

'Of course,' said Mrs Pargeter demurely, 'I have no idea what you're talking about. But I'm willing to be guided by you in such matters.' She turned the full beam of her violet-blue eyes on the computer expert. 'You're sure Chelmsford's the one, Jukebox?'

He nodded. 'Definitely the closest match to what's needed for this case.'

'Yeah,' Truffler agreed. 'Only the goods are different. Chelmsford was used fivers, this time it's paintings. Same basic strategy'd work, no problem.'

An infectious bubble of excitement was building up in all of them. It was comforting to have the quality of Jukebox Jarvis's archives to rely on. Inside his computer system every one of the late Mr Pargeter's greatest exploits was neatly catalogued and chronicled, providing a perfect template of action for any situation that could possibly arise. Many public companies would give half their annual profits for an infrastructure of such efficiency.

Mrs Pargeter spread the benison of her richest smile around the assembled company. 'Right, if you say so—Chelmsford it is.'

'Terrific,' said Jukebox, reaching forward to his computer. 'I'll print out the whole plan for you.' Gleefully, he touched a key and his printer burst into manic activity.

'This is great, isn't it?' Gary spoke for all of them. 'Almost like having Mr Pargeter back with us again.'

The other men grinned, but Mrs Pargeter, a trifle misty-eyed, murmured, 'Almost, Gary ... but not quite.'

Chapter Thirty-Two

A space had been cleared amidst the debris that littered Truffler Mason's desk, and over its surface was spread out a large-scale map of South London. Mrs Pargeter and the private investigator leant over, examining it minutely. Every now and then she would trace a little route with her finger, then consult the bound folder of neatly printed notes, plans and diagrams that Jukebox Jarvis had presented to her. Mrs Pargeter's hand would hover for a moment over each possible site, before finding some unconforming detail as a reason to reject it. Finally, her hand lingered longer over one particular network of junctions. She looked across at Truffler. 'How about *there?*'

He bent down from his great height and squinted at the map. 'Looks good.'

Mrs Pargeter double-checked with the requirements in her folder, before continuing, 'It's definitely the sort of loop road we're after—and there's the garage with a car wash.'

Truffler Mason nodded with that characteristic lethargy which, in his case, denoted huge enthusiasm. 'Right distance from the breaker's yard, and all. Couldn't be better.'

'Great.' Mrs Pargeter's enthusiasm never wore any disguise. It was, like most of her emotions, entirely transparent, fervent and joyous. 'You know,' she said with a delighted grin, 'I think I could get good at this.'

'You already are good at it, Mrs Pargeter,' said Truffler.

Gary's limousine cruised effortlessly through a leafy South London outer suburb, before coming to a stop, as an elderly lollipop man ushered some tiny anorak-swaddled schoolchildren over a crossing in the road. The man was so thin that, holding his round-topped staff, he looked like a stickman they might have drawn in class.

Gary pressed the button and the window slid soundlessly down. When his charges were safely on the other side of the road, the lollipop man waved an acknowledgement to the law-abiding driver. Then, as he recognized the face, his manner changed to one of great warmth and welcome.

'As I live and breathe ... Gary.'

The chauffeur stretched a hand out to shake the old man's bony fingers. 'Good to see you, mate. Mrs Pargeter—' he deferred to the plump, smiling woman in the back of the limousine, 'I'd like you to meet—Vanishing Vernon.'

'Delighted to make your acquaintance.' She stretched her hand through from the back. The old man clasped it in both of his. 'Oh, Mrs Pargeter ... Is it really you? You've no idea what an honour this is for me.'

From the glow on his face, you'd have thought he'd just been presented with an Oscar (though—thank God—he didn't make an acceptance speech).

Hedgeclipper Clinton's office at Greene's Hotel was decorated like an ante-room at Versailles. On its desk that afternoon was proudly displayed a portable television camera, firmly identified by the 'BBC-TV' logo. Kevin, one of the hotel's doormen, dressed in a black and gold uniform, looked on admiringly. The expression on Mrs Pargeter's face was more sceptical.

'Where did you get that from, Hedgeclipper?' she asked beadily.

He was squirming too much from embarrassment to pick her up on the use of his nickname in front of other hotel staff. 'Well ...' he prevaricated. 'I borrowed it.' He looked at Mrs Pargeter defensively. 'I'll take it back.' A look of righteousness came into his face as he thought of a justification for his actions. 'I do pay my TV licence fee, so by rights a bit of it's mine, anyway.'

'I see.' The violet-blue eyes held Hedgeclipper Clinton's for a long, wince-making moment before giving up on pointless recrimination and turning to the doorman. 'And you can manage with it all right, Kevin?'

He nodded complacently. 'No problem,

Mrs Pargeter. I've videoed all four of my mum's weddings.'

'Oh good.' She now beamed back at the hotel manager. Mrs Pargeter had never been one to bear grudges for any length of time. 'And you can do your bit, Hedgeclipper?'

'Mrs Pargeter,' he replied, almost offended by her doubting him, 'being a hotel manager is like being permanently in front of the camera.'

She nodded, then a shadow of anxiety crossed her usually sunny face. 'I hope this is going to work ...'

Hedgeclipper Clinton gave her a smile of confidence verging on complacency. 'I can assure you it will. It worked in Chelmsford, and on that occasion proved one great truth: You can never underestimate the mind-blowing stupidity of the British people when they're offered the chance to be on television.'

'True,' said Mrs Pargeter, reassured.

The space under the railway arch which had been converted into a body shop was dominated by a large van. Under floodlights, three mechanics were working on it. One, protected by goggles and gloves, was using an oxyacetylene lamp to cut a long slit in the vehicle's roof above the front seats. The second mechanic seemed only to possess a back end, the rest of his body buried, tinkering, under the bonnet; while the third was replacing the van's ordinary tyres with large thick-treaded ones. The bodywork was painted in a greyish undercoat.

Looking on, out of the glare of the floodlights, stood Hamish Ramon Henriques and Mrs Pargeter. She was once again holding the folder of printed notes she had received from Jukebox Jarvis.

'Going all right, is it?' she asked.

HRH flicked up his long moustaches with satisfaction. 'Absolutely as one would have wished. The engine in that beast's powerful enough for a tank.'

'Good. And the special paint job?'

'All in hand, Mrs Pargeter. Don't you worry.'

She caught his eye. She was enjoying this. Together they nodded, secure in their complicity.

One final preparation was required. It was made in the privacy of Jukebox Jarvis's front room. He had received his instructions over the phone from Truffler Mason, who had of course checked everything out with Mrs Pargeter beforehand.

It was a simple job by Jukebox's standards. All he had to do was hack into the police computer again (they'd had a rare flash of originality and, for the latest six-letter password, chosen 'arrest'). Once inside the system, he had to check up on the duty rosters for the next day.

What he found there was potentially worrying. The police had got hold of some information from somewhere. They were clearly getting suspicious about what Rod D'Acosta had in his yard. A raid on the place was planned for the following evening. To make matters worse, it was going to be headed up by one of the most ruthless and efficient detective inspectors in the Met.

A couple of clicks of the mouse and a few keyed-in words changed that. Within minutes, the efficient detective inspector was re-delegated to talk about Road Safety in an inner city primary school, and Inspector Wilkinson was in charge of the Rod D'Acosta investigation.

Then, just in case his new sidekick Hercule Hughes was as bright as the evidence suggested he might be, the Sergeant's schedule was also adjusted. He was diverted to Heathrow Airport to control the horde of teenyboppers awaiting the arrival of the flight carrying the latest pop sensation, Boymeetzgirl.

Mrs Pargeter had always been in favour of celebration. Pampering when on her own was very important to her, and the good efforts of others never went unrewarded either. So, after all the planning and preparation they had put in, it seemed entirely logical that she should invite Truffler Mason, HRH, Gary, Jukebox Jarvis, Hedgeclipper Clinton, Kevin the doorman and Vanishing Vernon to a lavish dinner at Greene's Hotel.

All were smartly dressed. Mrs Pargeter was wearing a new creation, a flowing silk number in a strident red a lesser woman could not have got away with. Specially for the occasion, she had taken out of the hotel safe the diamond choker and bracelet whose owner, before the late Mr Pargeter had decided they'd suit his adored wife, had ruled many of the United Arab

Emirates. Mrs Pargeter herself looked as sparkly as the jewels.

Her party having given the Greene's Hotel wine list an exhaustive workout, at the end of the meal had homed back in on champagne. Not the most expensive on the list—Mrs Pargeter never believed in extravagance—but one whose vintage she knew to be reliable.

After a waiter had once again recharged all their glasses, Mrs Pargeter raised hers to her guests. 'Right, gentlemen. Good luck to all of you for tomorrow.'

'Yes,' said Truffler. 'And let's just all pray it doesn't rain. It's been sheeting down the last couple of days. And rain could really screw things up for us.'

'Don't worry.' Mrs Pargeter rested a reassuring hand on his sleeve. 'Forecast says tomorrow's going to be a beautiful day.' Waving her glass towards them, she announced, 'So, the toast is ...' She waited till all their glasses were raised to meet hers. 'Chelmsford Two—the Sequel!'

There was an enthusiastic clinking as the seven male voices echoed, 'Chelmsford Two—the Sequel!'

Then there was an equally enthusiastic slurping of champagne.

Chapter Thirty-Three

Inspector Wilkinson went into his office the next morning without enthusiasm. Attempts to interview Veronica Chastaigne had not met with success. She was still in hospital and the consultant in charge said she was far too frail to submit to any kind of questioning. When she had recovered, of course, there would be no problem. But the way the consultant said this implied slender hopes that she was ever going to recover.

So Wilkinson felt he was up against a brick wall. This sense had been exacerbated by a meeting the day before with his immediate superior, the 'jumped-up, university-educated, pen-pushing desk-driver', with whom the Inspector, like all good coppers, didn't get on. His Superintendent reckoned that the arrest of Reginald Winthrop represented a result, and that therefore no further investigation was required into the series of art thefts. Wilkinson was off the case.

To rub salt in the wound, the Superintendent had also somehow found out the part that Sergeant Hughes had played in events at Dover, and was putting the young man's name forward for some kind of commendation.

So Wilkinson approached work that day in a low mood. But for one tiny spark of a distant thought glowing in his mind, he would have been very depressed indeed. He knew for sure that the next couple of days would be depressing. Concentrating on the art thefts had spared him other, more tedious jobs, but now that he was off the case, his boss was going to ensure that he got the most tedious available.

That day he was down to give a lecture on Road Safety at an inner city primary school. The last officer who'd been landed with that number had come back having had his wallet stolen, his eye blacked by a stone that had been thrown at him, and with the left-hand side of his car sprayed fluorescent green.

But when Inspector Wilkinson actually looked at the printout of the daily roster, he could hardly believe his eyes. Could hardly believe his luck either. The Road Safety duty had been apportioned to one of the toughest and most successful inspectors in the unit, a man who was on record as saying, with considerable frequency, 'School visits are for braindead wimps.'

While he, Craig Wilkinson, had been given instead one of the most attractive assignments for years.

It was a raid on a suspicious breaker's yard, where stolen goods were thought to be hidden. And the yard was believed to belong to Rod D'Acosta, a South London villain on whom they'd been trying for years to get enough evidence to make a conviction stick.

This was terrific news for Wilkinson. The operation would involve taking a large squad of men, some of them armed. It would make him, as their leader, look impressive, while putting him at minimal personal risk. It would involve bulletproof vests, searchlights and lots of shouting through loudspeakers. It was the kind of rare job opportunity, the chance to play cops 'n' robbers, for which Inspector Wilkinson—and indeed most of his colleagues—had joined the Police Force.

He turned away from the printout, then had another, rather dampening thought.

Was this wonderful assignment destined to be spoiled, like so much of what he'd done over the previous two weeks, by the presence of Sergeant Hughes?

But no. Wilkinson's luck held. More than held, it was very good. The list told him that, instead of the odious Hughes, he'd been allocated the support of a new female detective sergeant, who'd been the subject of much ribald suggestion and erotic aspiration in the canteen.

Inspector Wilkinson preened his moustache, which wasn't growing as quickly as he'd hoped it would. That didn't worry him at that moment, though, because he was thinking of the female DS. She'd be really impressed when she saw him masterminding the raid on Rod D'Acosta's yard. She couldn't fail to look on him with respect after the operation was completed. Yes, he might be in with a chance there. Power, he knew, was a great aphrodisiac.

To complete his euphoria, Wilkinson saw that Sergeant Hughes had been allocated to one of the real short-straw duties. Policing teenyboppers at Heathrow. What was known round the station as a 'not a dry seat in the house' patrol.

Tee-hee. Serve the cocky little smart-arse bloody well right.

Wilkinson went to check the details of the D'Acosta operation with the detectives who'd been working on it. They seemed rather miffed that, after all the graft their regular inspector had put in setting the raid up, he was not scheduled to complete the job. Still, they couldn't argue with the roster and, with varying degrees of bad grace, they gave Wilkinson the information he required.

It was perfect. Surveillance from four in the afternoon, then slam in hard at around eight when it was dark. Going through the stuff in the yard'd take an hour top-weight. There'd still be time for Inspector Wilkinson to go to the pub near the station afterwards to accept the plaudits of his inferiors.

To build himself up for the day ahead, he went down to the canteen to wallow in the grease of an All-Day Breakfast.

It was while he was sitting there over his congealing eggs that a pale shadow of recollection crossed Inspector Wilkinson's sunny mood. He found himself thinking back, as he so often did, to the one big failure of his life. The biggest failure. The moment when he had been so close to success and when his plans had suddenly gone pear-shaped.

He had built everything up, prepared the whole operation in his customary painstaking way. He'd tested every stage of his plan for weaknesses and he'd felt ridiculously, headily confident that it was going to work. This was to be the moment when he, Detective Inspector Craig Wilkinson, made his mark on the British Police Force.

He had been all set to arrest Mr Pargeter, and then bring in the shoals of smaller fish who travelled in the master criminal's wake. The Inspector's triumph seemed assured. His was an operation that would continue to be talked about in awestruck voices round the Met for years to come.

The memory of how it had all gone wrong could still bring a cold shiver to Wilkinson's spine. Even he sometimes felt a bit of a fool about it.

He tried never to think about the incident. He'd certainly drive miles out of his way to avoid passing through the place where it had happened. And if he heard the town mentioned on the radio or television news, it still gave him an unpleasant little *frisson.*

Yes, it would be a long time before Detective Inspector Craig Wilkinson forgot the name of Chelmsford.

Chapter Thirty-Four

The red Transit was still inside the fortified breaker's yard, but it didn't look as if it would be there for much longer. Rod D'Acosta and two of his heavies emerged from their hut and crossed towards the van. They had received orders to move out that morning. But just as Rod's hand reached to open the passenger-side door, his attention was attracted by something happening in the street outside, and he moved closer to the gates to get a better look.

Apparently a television programme was being made. A man with a portable BBC-TV camera was filming another man with an oleaginous smile and odious leisurewear. As always, the scene had attracted its little knot of gawping viewers, fascinated by being close to the manufacture of the

226

country's favourite medium.

The man in the odious leisurewear seemed to be recording some direct-to-camera links. He stood in front of the wall of a house, on which a huge poster had been plastered, and fixed his unctuous smile on the camera lens. The links evidently recorded to his satisfaction, he redirected the beam of his unctuousness to the growing crowd.

'Now listen, everybody,' he smarmed, 'we've set up a stunt here for Saturday night's programme.' At this news his audience giggled in witless anticipation. 'We're going to get some unsuspecting member of the public to look a right idiot and we're going to film them so that everyone at home can have a good laugh.' His audience roared at the prospect of such hilarity. 'Just like we do every Saturday. Isn't that right, Kevin?'

The cameraman, chuckling to demonstrate what a good sport and how much part of the joke he was, agreed, 'Yes, that's right, Des.'

Rod D'Acosta, inside the gates of his yard, chuckled too, and waved two of his henchmen across. 'Hey, Ray, Phil! They're doing one of those daft telly stunts over there.'

The two heavies who'd suffered such a rude awakening in their car a few nights before, lumbered across to check out what their boss was talking about.

'Oh yeah?' said the heavy called Ray.

'Who's the geezer fronting it?' asked the heavy called Phil.

The correct answer to this question was Hedgeclipper Clinton, but Rod D'Acosta couldn't have been expected to know that. 'Looks familiar,' he said. 'Can't remember his name, though. I get all those blokes on the telly mixed up.'

The heavy called Phil pushed open the gates of the yard. 'Lets go and have a butcher's then, eh?'

All three men moved forward to join the periphery of the crowd, amongst whose number they did not recognize Truffler Mason or Gary the chauffeur. And, like their boss, Ray and Phil didn't know that the presenter with a permanent nudge in his voice was Hedgeclipper Clinton, as he went on, '... and, though it looks as if the wall's perfectly solid, in fact behind the poster there's nothing there and somebody would be able to walk straight through it!'

The crowd, including Rod D'Acosta and his two heavies, oohed and tittered at the daring wit of this concept. Inside the yard, the remaining heavy, whose name was Sid, was drawn by the noise and moved slowly towards the open gates. Sid was the heaviest of all the heavies, and big with it.

'But,' Hedgeclipper went on mischievously, 'who'll be caught in the stunt? That's what we want to know, isn't it? I'm going to offer fifty pounds to someone to walk straight into that wall.'

Rod D'Acosta, always quick to recognize that fifty pounds was indeed fifty pounds, immediately volunteered. 'Can I have a go?'

'No, of course you can't,' the presenter replied in exasperation, 'because you know what's going to happen. We've got to find someone who doesn't realize it's a set-up. We'll try the trick out on the next unsuspecting passer-by who comes along.'

The crowd giggled delightedly at the prospect of a fellow human being's imminent humiliation. But, as they looked up and down the street, their giggles died away. There was no one in sight. Why was it, they mused with irritation, that just when you need a patsy, there's never one around?

A tall, mournful-looking man in the crowd turned to Rod D'Acosta and his two heavies. He indicated the one called Sid, still lingering, fascinated but out of earshot, by the yard gates. 'Why not ask your mate over there? He doesn't know what's going to happen, does he?'

Rod caught on straight away. 'True.' He shouted across, 'Here, Sid. You want to make fifty quid and be on the telly?'

Sid lumbered across to join them willingly enough, but a look of suspicion had overspread his Neanderthal features. 'What you say, Rod? What's the catch?'

His answer came from the presenter. With a smile that plumbed new depths of unctuousness, Hedgeclipper Clinton said, 'There is no catch, sir.' He gestured to his cameraman. 'OK, roll, Kevin.' The presenter pointed up to the poster-covered wall and fixed his expression of professional *bonhomie* in place. 'This, as you see, is a perfectly ordinary wall.' He focused the rictus of his grin on the heavy called Sid. 'Now, sir, are you the kind of gentleman who normally walks into walls?'

'Course not.'

The audience tittered at this Wildean exchange.

'But, sir, would you walk into a wall for *fifty pounds* ...?'

This exchange between presenter and patsy, and the delicious prospect of someone shortly being made to look a fool, exercised their customary magnetism on the British public. Every eye was focused on the two men standing in front of the poster-covered wall. So nobody noticed when the tall, lugubrious man and another, shorter one detached themselves from the fringes of the crowd and sauntered unobtrusively across towards the gates of the breaker's yard.

'Might think about it,' said Sid, responding to the presenter's appeal to his greed.

'Particularly if I guaranteed that you wouldn't hurt yourself ...?'

'Well ...'

'Go on,' Hedgeclipper Clinton urged seductively, and then he brought up the clinching argument that would have persuaded almost anyone in the country to do anything. 'You have a chance to appear on television. Don't you want to show the people at home what a good sport you are?'

Urged on by shouts from the crowd and his own instinct that, given an opening, he could show some of those professional TV smoothies a thing or two, Sid put on his best smile and ran a comb of fingers through his thinning hair. 'Yeah, go on,' he said in his 'good sport' voice. 'I'm game for anything.'

'Great!' the ecstatic presenter cried. 'What a lovely person you are!' He pulled five ten-pound notes out of his pocket, and the crowd who, like all television audiences, will always applaud money and consumer durables, cheered and stamped their feet in the excitement of the occasion.

'See, there it is,' Hedgeclipper went on, 'fifty pounds if you'll trust me, take my word for it when I say you won't get hurt and ... walk into that wall!'

'OK,' said Sid who, in his imagination, had just collected the Most Popular TV Personality Award for the fifth year running.

With a cheery grin into Kevin the doorman's camera, Sid gathered his energies and made as if to sprint towards the false wall.

'Ooh,' the presenter cried, with an unfailing instinct for what makes good television. 'Is he actually going to *run* into it for us?'

'You bet!' replied Sid, whose imagined television career had just started to take off in the States.

To ever rising cheers from his audience—and ever rising career expectations in his imagination—Sid the heavy launched himself forward and sprinted towards the poster. Showing good professional instincts, he flashed a smile at Kevin the doorman's camera just the moment before he hit the poster and, as he expected, burst through it into the void.

That wasn't what happened, however. Behind the poster there was no void. There was nothing except for a solid brick wall, into which Sid smashed with all the velocity of his eighteen-stone body.

The cheers of the audience trickled to nothing as, clutching at his face, Sid the heavy tottered back from the wall. But suddenly the focus of attention shifted away from him. It was drawn by the sound of a vehicle's engine starting.

The crowd turned as one to see the red Transit surge out through the yard's open gates. While they gaped uncomprehendingly, the van's back doors were opened by Truffler Mason. Hedge-clipper Clinton and Kevin the doorman, who'd been ready for this moment, jumped inside. The doors swung shut again, as Gary gunned the engine and the red Transit screeched off into the distance.

'Oi!' screamed Rod D'Acosta 'They got the stuff!'

'Come on!' shouted the heavy called Ray.

While he, Rod and the heavy called Phil fought their way through the confused crowd back to their yard, the heavy called Sid slipped quietly to the ground at the foot of the wall, where he lay with an extremely stupid grin on his face. ''Ere!' he demanded in the moment before he lost consciousness. 'Where's my fifty quid?'

Chapter Thirty-Five

There's only so much you can do at Heathrow Airport, as Sergeant Hughes was finding out, to his considerable annoyance. The flight on which pop sensation Boymeetzgirl were arriving from their tour of Poland had been delayed by two hours, and the Sergeant was bored stiff.

Also it looked as if the whole policing operation was going to be entirely unnecessary. Boymeetzgirl were evidently not quite as big a pop sensation as their record company's publicity department had puffed them up to be. The promised hordes of uncontrollable teenyboppers which prompted the police presence had not materialized. Maybe a dozen smallish girls with braces on their teeth, headphones on their ears and incipient puberty on the other parts of their bodies, clustered round the Arrivals gate, bearing hand-scrawled Boymeetzgirl banners. Rioting and public affray did not look to be on the cards.

Sergeant Hughes felt very frustrated. Like Inspector Wilkinson, he had been told that, following the arrest of Reg Winthrop, the arts theft investigation was at an end. It had progressed as far as it could. Hughes didn't believe this. To his mind they'd just lifted up a corner of the carpet on that one, and considerable riches lay yet to be discovered. They'd hardly started.

Hughes was also frustrated by the knowledge that Inspector Wilkinson had been scheduled for a much more appealing assignment. The raid on Rod D'Acosta's breaker's yard sounded real fun. It would undoubtedly involve bullet-proof vests, searchlights and lots of shouting through loudspeakers. It was exactly the sort of shooty-bang opportunity for which Sergeant Hercule Hughes had joined the Police Force.

Why a juicy job of that sort should go to a useless old dinosaur like Wilkinson, Hughes could not begin to imagine. It was the sort of assignment that should go to a young Turk, someone with a bit of style, someone with charisma. To him, in fact.

Yes, he wasn't going to be Sergeant Hughes for long. Once he presented the Superintendent with the completed dossier he'd been building up on the laptop in his flat, fast-track promotion would be a certainty.

Hughes'd had a cup of coffee, he'd read all the newspaper headlines in the bookshop, he'd decided he didn't want to buy any ties, smoked salmon or inflatable travel cushions, and his boredom was getting deeper by the minute. He looked at his watch. Still an hour and a half before the rescheduled flight from Warsaw was due to arrive. That was assuming there wasn't another delay.

For something to do, he got out his mobile phone and dialled his home number. Check the answering machine, see if there were any messages. He wasn't optimistic. There was no way the dumped long-standing girlfriend in Sheffield was going to ring him, and he had yet to develop much of a social life in London. (He did have plans in this direction, though. Once he'd got his career established, then he'd sort out his sex life. In his view, London's lucky women didn't know what was about to hit them.) But his current lack of a social life was another reason why he liked working on his days off. It was something to do.

To his surprise, the machine indicated there was a message for him. He played it back, casual interest quickly giving way to mounting excitement.

It was an educated voice, which spoke with little intonation. 'Hello, Sergeant Hughes. This is another message from Posey Narker, who tipped you off about the Dover smuggling attempt. Congratulations on following up on that. I must say, after years of giving information to Inspector

Wilkinson, it's a relief to be dealing with someone who seems to have a bit of intelligence.

'I have more information for you about the Pargeter set-up. Mr Pargeter, as I'm sure you know, is dead, but some of his old accomplices are banding up again to perpetrate a major art theft. This morning they will be hijacking a lorry full of stolen paintings from a breaker's yard owned by a villain called Rod D'Acosta. It is situated at ...'

Sergeant Hughes continued listening to the address as he broke into a run towards the car park. Never mind about Boymeetzgirl. Their frenzied fans could tear the whole airport apart so far as he was concerned. Hercule Hughes had bigger fish to fry.

Chapter Thirty-Six

The van which Mrs Pargeter had last seen in the body shop painted grey was now painted blue. She sat in the passenger seat, with Hamish Ramon Henriques at

238

the wheel beside her. They were parked in the network of streets that Mrs Pargeter and Truffler had selected as ideal for their operation. HRH's fingers drummed lightly on the steering wheel; Mrs Pargeter hummed softly. Both were tense, but tense with excitement rather than anxiety.

At the sound of a fast-approaching vehicle, HRH came to life. 'Here we go,' he murmured.

As he and Mrs Pargeter got out of their van, the red Transit screeched to a halt behind them, then reversed up, so that the backs of the two vehicles faced each other, some five metres apart. At the moment Mrs Pargeter and HRH opened the back doors of their van, the Transit's swung wide to reveal Truffler, Hedgeclipper Clinton and Kevin the doorman. As Gary appeared from the driver's door, Truffler and Kevin jumped down into the space between the two vans. Truffler turned to receive the first painting from Hedgeclipper, passed it to Kevin, who passed it to Gary who handed it up to HRH, who in turn stowed it in the back of the blue van.

Mrs Pargeter looked on with quiet pride,

as the complete transfer of goods was achieved within ninety seconds. The last to be safely packed away was a rather soulful Raphael Madonna.

At the moment Hamish Ramon Henriques slotted the painting into place, Mrs Pargeter turned towards the sound of approaching cars. 'Just in time. Close both sets of doors and into the blue van!'

She and Gary bundled into the front seats, the rest climbed into the back, pulling the doors shut behind them.

Seconds later, two cars full of heavies screamed up. The heavy called Ray drove one. The other, with Rod D'Acosta in the passenger seat, was driven by the heavy called Phil. (The heavy called Sid was still blissfully unconscious at the foot of the wall he'd run into.) The cars passed the blue van and homed in on the red Transit. One slid into the space across which the paintings had been passed, and came to rest with its bumper touching the van's back doors; the other backed up till it was parked in contact with the van's front grille. There was no way the Transit could get out of that pincer movement.

Nonchalantly, confident their quarry was trapped, Rod D'Acosta and his two heavies got out of their vehicles. Carrying an array of baseball bats and pickaxe handles, they moved menacingly forward.

At the very second they looked into the cab of the Transit and realized it was empty, the engine of the other van was detonated into action. The chief villain and his two henchmen turned in dismay to watch its blue back doors diminishing away down the street.

'Get back in,' Rod D'Acosta bawled in fury, 'and turn the bloody cars round!'

The blue van and its two pursuing cars hurtled through the streets of South London, dropping the jaws of passers-by and threatening the heart conditions of other road-users. In spite of the van's souped-up engine, the superior power of the cars was beginning to tell. They were gaining on their quarry.

In the van's passenger seat Mrs Pargeter, who had been tracing their route across the map on her lap, shouted suddenly, 'This is it. Swing a left, Gary.'

The blue van did as instructed, the suddenness of the swing forcing its whole weight momentarily on to two wheels. But it righted itself and roared off down the side road.

The pursuing cars slowed, and the one behind eased up alongside its leader. Windows were wound down. Rod D'Acosta grinned wolfishly across the intervening space to the heavy called Ray. 'Got them now,' he announced. 'This road's just a loop. You head them off the other end.'

'Right,' said the heavy called Ray, and fired his car forward to block off the junction ahead. Rod D'Acosta nodded to the heavy called Phil, who turned his car down the side road and moved sedately ahead. There was no hurry now. The blue van was trapped as securely as the red one had been. They could move slowly, relishing the thought of the inevitable violence which lay ahead.

Halfway along the loop road was a service station. The blue van hurtled across its forecourt, straight towards the car wash at the back. It stopped by the control slot.

'You got a token?' asked Gary, as he wound his window down.

'Course I have,' replied Mrs Pargeter, almost offended that he thought the question necessary. 'Full Wash with Wheel Scrub.'

She handed it across. Gary pushed the token into the slot and, winding his window up, edged forward, guided by rails, into the car wash. The overhead sprays of water started, and moved slowly back over the blue van's body.

As they did so, something remarkable happened. The blue paint stippled, paled and trickled away down the van's sides into the car-wash gutters, revealing gleaming white gloss beneath.

By the time the wheel scrub, the final feature of the cleaning cycle, was finished, not a trace of blue remained anywhere on the gleaming body. Had there been anyone present to witness the colour transformation, as Gary inched the van primly out of the car wash, they would also have noticed that he and Mrs Pargeter were now wearing navy-blue jackets and caps.

And at the moment the conjectural observer noticed the word 'Ambulance' printed on the front of the cab, they would have seen a slot in the roof open, and an array of blue flashing lights rise up to fill it. Simultaneously, as the vehicle sped forward on to the road, they would have heard an emergency siren start.

The heavy called Ray had his car parked directly across the outlet of the loop road to the main thoroughfare. And he wasn't going to let anything out.

Except of course for an ambulance. You never knew with an ambulance. The geezer in the back whose life was at risk could be a cop, true. But, on the other hand, it could be one of your own. Better to be safe than sorry.

So, at the sound of the siren and the sight of the flashing blue lights, the heavy called Ray edged his car out of the way. Once the ambulance had passed, he moved back to block the roadway once again.

Then he sat and waited.

He waited a long time. All the time until a familiar car came slowly out of the loop road. Behind its windscreen the heavy called Ray could see a familiar face. It belonged to Rod D'Acosta, and it was suffused with a familiar expression of fury.

Chapter Thirty-Seven

'It's gone!' Sergeant Hughes announced dramatically, as their car drew up outside the open metal gates.

'Now just a minute, just a minute. Don't let's jump to conclusions. We don't know what we're looking for yet.' Inspector Wilkinson didn't like being rushed in this manner. The raid on Rod D'Acosta's yard was his assignment and he had planned to start on it at four o'clock in the afternoon. He had not responded well to Hughes's melodramatic intervention and insistence on moving the whole schedule forward.

'We do know what we're looking for. It's a red Transit van, and it's not here.' Then, as an almost condescending afterthought, the Sergeant added, 'Sir.'

'Where did you say you got this information from?'

'The source called Posey Narker who put me on to the Dover thing.' Hughes reached forward to the car phone. 'I've got the van's registration. I'll put out a general alert. We'll track it down.'

Wilkinson snatched the receiver from his hand and started punching in a number. '*I'll* put out a general alert, thank you very much. And *I'll* track it down.' He got through. 'General alert for a red Transit in the South London area.' He turned testily to the Sergeant. 'What's the registration, Hughes?'

While the Inspector gave details into the phone, Sergeant Hughes became aware of a large man behaving strangely on the other side of the road. He was weaving around, as if in a daze, with an expression of deep puzzlement on his bruised face.

Hughes got out of the car, and went across to the man. 'Are you all right?'

The eyes of the heavy called Sid took a moment or two to focus on the young man in front of him. ''Ere. Have you got my fifty quid?' he asked in a slurred voice.

'No, I haven't. What happened to you?'

'Well, I ran into this wall, didn't I?'

'Ah. Why?'

'To get the fifty quid.'

'Oh.'

'Are you sure you haven't got it?'

'Absolutely certain.'

'Oh.'

The big man looked almost pitifully disappointed. Sergeant Hughes got out his notebook. 'Can I just take a few details about you? What's your name?'

'Sid,' the man replied uncertainly. 'I think.'

'And what do you do?'

His fuddled state removed the normal caution with which he would have replied to such a question. 'I work for Rod D'Acosta. Threatening and GBH, mostly. Occasionally a bit of petty theft.'

'Right,' said Sergeant Hughes, wishing that all arrests were as easy as this one promised to be. 'I think you'd better come along with me.'

The two cars were parked on the service station forecourt. The knot of three men stood with heads bowed. They could have been attending a funeral, but it wasn't a grave they were looking down at, just the traces of blue pigment in the gutters of a car wash.

Rod D'Acosta shook his head ruefully.

'It was the ambulance ...?' asked the heavy called Ray.

But the question was a formality. He knew the answer.

'Yes, you bloody fool, it was the ambulance!' said the heavy called Phil. 'The ambulance that you so public-spiritedly allowed to drive straight past you!'

'It wasn't my bleedin' fault. I wasn't to know that—'

'Ssh ...' Rod D'Acosta was too distracted to join in their bickering, too distracted even to give a personal carpeting to the heavy called Ray. He looked down at the blue-stained gutter and shook his head once again. 'You know, I haven't heard of this stroke being pulled since ...'

The heavy called Phil breathed the word, 'Chelmsford ...?'

'Yes,' Rod D'Acosta confirmed.

'Oh, my good Gawd!' said the heavy called Ray on a note of panic. 'Mr Pargeter hasn't come back to life, has he?'

It didn't take Inspector Wilkinson and Sergeant Hughes long to find the abandoned red Transit. And it didn't take them long to establish that the van was empty.

'What do you reckon they've done?' Hughes asked the befuddled man in the back of their car.

'Dunno,' said the heavy called Sid.

248

'Probably transferred the loot to another van. Or one of their cars, possibly.'

'Could you give us the registration numbers?'

The heavy called Sid did as requested. Sergeant Hughes proffered the car phone politely to his boss. 'Would you like to put out a general alert, sir?'

With bad grace, Wilkinson took the phone and keyed in the number.

While his boss gave instructions to base, Hughes turned again to the man in the back. 'What was the loot in the Transit, as a matter of interest?'

'Paintings. Old paintings, you know. Stuff we nicked from an old house called Chastaigne Varleigh.'

This was terrific. It seemed there were no beans the bewildered man was not prepared to spill. Hughes gleefully envisaged another crime dossier, to match the one he was building up on the late Mr Pargeter. Confident that imminent promotion was a certainty, he pressed home his advantage. 'Who actually nicked the stuff?'

'Me and Rod D'Acosta.'

'Can you give me details of any other jobs you've done with him?'

'Oh *yes,*' the heavy called Sid replied, and proceeded to rattle off a long catalogue, all of which Sergeant Hughes transcribed into his notebook.

Chapter Thirty-Eight

The ambulance was now bowling cheerfully through the open Surrey countryside. Its siren and lights had been switched off, and Mrs Pargeter was leading her male voice choir in singing 'All Things Bright and Beautiful'.

They'd just got to

The rich man in his castle,
The poor man at his gate,

when she noticed a crudely painted roadside sign: 'CAR BOOT SALE—ONE MILE.

'Nearly there,' cried Mrs Pargeter. 'Ooh, I must just make a phone call.' She reached for the phone and dialled the number that Inspector Wilkinson had given her. She didn't identify herself, but gave him a few terse words of information.

She ended the call, beamed cheerily and picked up again with the hymn.

God made them, high or lowly,
And ordered their estate.

In his car as it sped through the lanes of Surrey the heavy called Phil seemed to have caught the anxiety of the heavy called Ray from the car behind. 'You don't think Mr Pargeter really is back alive again, do you, Rod?'

'Of course he bloody isn't! He died years back. I sent a couple of my men to his funeral to make sure he was good and buried.'

'But you don't know what was in the coffin, do you?'

'For Christ's sake! Mr Pargeter is dead! Dead, dead, dead! No one will ever see him in the flesh again—all right?'

'All right,' the heavy called Phil conceded grudgingly. Then, after a silence, he asked, 'Rod ... you don't believe in ghosts, do you?'

'Of course I don't bloody believe in bloody ghosts! Now will you drive this bloody car a bit bloody faster!'

The car boot sale was being held in a grassy field which abutted ploughed land beyond. Either side of a wide aisle a large number of cars was parked facing outward. A tatty mixture of goods were displayed on picnic tables in front of their open boots and hatchbacks. Large numbers of potential purchasers ambled up and down the aisle, convinced they were going to find bargains.

As the ambulance turned off the road into the field, Mrs Pargeter suffered an uncharacteristic moment of self-doubt. 'I hope Vanishing Vernon's done his stuff,' she murmured to Gary.

'He will have, don't you worry.'

'Yes, yes, of course he will.' Reassured, she looked into the back of the van. 'How're you getting on, Truffler?'

With a mournful flourish, the private investigator stuck a printed label on to a neatly wrapped rectangular package. 'Fine, Mrs Pargeter,' he replied. 'That's the last one. All the paintings labelled up, marked with where they got to go back to.'

'Terrific. Veronica Chastaigne will be pleased.'

A mile behind, the car carrying Rod D'Acosta passed the sign to the car boot sale. 'We'll get them now!' he hissed viciously.

'Yes ...' The heavy called Phil didn't sound as convinced as his boss. 'Are you sure there aren't such things as ghosts, Rod ...?'

'Do you recognize that car ahead?' asked Sergeant Hughes.

'Yes,' the heavy called Sid replied. 'That's Rod's all right. It's the one he used for the getaway from the Peckham Rye bank job.'

Hughes wished he wasn't driving, so that he could make more notes on this valuable flood of information.

'The car's going exactly where my informant said it would,' Inspector Wilkinson observed smugly. That call on his mobile couldn't have been better timed. Of course it had been pure luck that the Inspector had received information about Rod D'Acosta's movements at such a relevant moment, but he wasn't going to let Hughes know that.

Oh no. Wilkinson had made it appear

that the call was part of some masterplan held been working on for weeks. Sergeant Hughes had been well impressed.

That'll show the cocky little oik, thought Wilkinson. Complacently, he stroked the line of his growing moustache.

Ushered along by the stick-like figure of Vanishing Vernon, almost like the man with the red flag who had to precede early motor cars, the ambulance moved serenely down the long aisle of open car boots. Car boot shoppers turned to look curiously as, from the back doors, Truffler Mason handed out labelled rectangular packages to HRH, Hedgeclipper Clinton and Kevin the doorman. These were then passed on to the owners of the parked cars.

As each owner received his or her picture, they checked its destination on the label and put it in their car boot, which was then firmly closed. No attempt was made to remove the picnic tables loaded with bric-à-brac, as, to the considerable confusion of the shoppers, the owners got into their cars and began to drive away out of the field.

But, before the first of them reached the exit to the main road, Rod D'Acosta's two cars came hurtling in at great speed. Car boot shoppers scattered in panic as the vehicles thundered side by side down the wide aisle in pursuit of the ambulance.

Truffler Mason, who had just handed out the last package, saw the approaching cars, slammed the doors of the ambulance shut, and called out, 'All done!'

'Go for it, Gary!' shouted Mrs Pargeter, with a note of sheer devilment in her voice.

The chauffeur put his foot down, pointing the ambulance straight at the open gate which led to the ploughed fields beyond. The mud was thick and sticky from recent rain, but the supercharged engine's power took over and the vehicle surged across the ridges, riding high and untrammelled on its special tyres.

Rod D'Acosta's two cars started the pursuit, but didn't get far in the treacly mud of the ploughed field. Just inside the gate, the cars' wheels started to spin and their bodies to slew dangerously sideways.

The two vehicles cannoned into each other with a sickening clang. There was a crunching of glass and the impact made both of their boots fly open.

Urged on by Vanishing Vernon, the car boot shoppers surged forward to see what new treasures were on offer. As Rod D'Acosta and his dazed acolytes staggered out of their ruined cars, they found themselves faced by a crowd of bargain-hunters, keen to know how much they were asking for the knuckledusters, bowie knives and Armalite rifles in their boots.

It was at that moment that the car containing Inspector Wilkinson, Sergeant Hughes and the heavy called Sid arrived.

Chapter Thirty-Nine

It was an ordinary morning for the security guard of the Kunsthistorisches Museum in Düsseldorf. As usual there was a dull ache inside the top of his skull. As usual he regretted having that extra beer the previous evening. And as usual the residue of the bratwurst, which had been so delicious the night before, didn't taste so good on his morning tongue.

Still, there was work to be done. Maybe he'd be able to slip out for another beer at lunchtime. That'd make him feel better.

He keyed in the relevant code at the side door of the museum's impressive frontage, and waited till the night security guard let him in. He checked through the night security guard's log and went to open up the galleries. Every painting had to be checked, every alarm tested, in the hour before the day's throng of culture lovers was admitted.

He keyed in the seven-digit code which unlocked the tall doors leading to the Medieval and Old Master series of galleries. The doors swung open, he fixed them back on their hooks, then turned to face the familiar outlines of Madonnas and martyrdoms. He didn't know much about art, but he knew whereabouts on the walls it all belonged.

Everything was exactly where it should have been until he entered the High Renaissance Gallery. This was usually one of the quickest visits in his tour of inspection. Since the famous 1982 robbery, there was embarrassingly less to display than there should have been. The remaining paintings—all minor works by lesser artists (the thieves had known precisely what they were looking for)—had been rehung and there had been some buying at major auctions to fill the space, but there was still too much blank wall for comfort.

The security guard flicked an eye over the few familiar works and was about to move on when he caught sight of something unexpected and looked down. Propped along the bottom of one of the gallery walls were five paintings. Even though he knew little about art, the museum robbery had received so much media coverage back in 1982 that anyone in the country would have recognized them. The Uccello was there, the Piero della Francesca, the two Titians. Above all, there was the famous Leonardo.

The security guard let out a little belch of surprise. The bratwurst taste in his mouth was more pungent than ever.

Neatly attached to the top of the Leonardo was a little note. In perfect German it read: 'THANKS FOR THE LOAN OF THESE.'

Dealing with a client of Mr Takachi's eminence was not something that could be delegated to a minor official; this was a job for the bank's Vice-President. With elaborate courtesy the appointed Vice-

President escorted the honoured customer to the lift which led down to the New York bank's vaults.

On the basement level he checked his ID with the uniformed guard, who keyed in the appropriate code to open the heavy metal doors guarding the galleries of neatly ranked security boxes.

Another uniformed guard accompanied them inside. Attached by a chain to his metal waistband was the second key which had to be turned at the same moment as the key the Vice-President carried if the box was to be opened.

'And it's just the pearls you want to take out for the moment?' asked the Vice-President.

Mr Takachi nodded acknowledgement of this. 'I am taking my wife to the Pearl Harbor Apology Ball at the White House. Very prestigious occasion. Fundraising event for Democratic Party.'

'Ah,' said the Vice-President. 'Right.' He stopped in front of one particular security box and looked at the uniformed guard. 'Ready with your key?'

The man nodded. 'Now we have to turn them absolutely together,' the Vice-President continued. 'If we're out of synch, the alarm goes off straight away, the doors close automatically and we're locked in. It's just another of our security measures,' he added to Mr Takachi, who bowed.

With the keys in place, the two men, watching each other's hands, turned together. The thick, nuclearblast-proof door swung outward.

Inside the security box were visible neat piles of gold bars, stacks of document cases, terraces of jewel boxes. Looking sternly down on them from the back was a gold-framed picture of a white-ruffed burgomaster.

'Aah,' said Mr Takachi delightedly. 'You found my Rembrandt!'

Nestling amidst the Highlands of Scotland there is a grey stone castle, turreted like a fantasy from a fairy tale. Its grounds stretch far in every direction, encompassing forests and glens, moorland and twinkling lochs. Broad-antlered stags roam through its wildness; plump grouse nest in its lush undergrowth.

On the same day that the security guard found the Old Master in Düsseldorf, and that Mr Takachi was reunited with his Rembrandt in New York, the studded oak front door of the Scottish castle opened, and the eleventh Duke emerged into the misty morning. He wore a threadbare tartan dressing gown and an expression of disgruntlement. The eleventh Duke was of the view—particularly first thing in the morning—that during his lifetime everything had changed for the worse. You couldn't get staff these days; the only sorts of people who could afford to run stately homes were rock stars, press barons and comparable forms of pond life; and young people had no respect for tradition.

He sniffed the unfailing freshness of the Highland air, and stretched out his creaking arms. Then he looked down to the broad doorstep for the morning's delivery.

The usual order was there—one bottle of silver-topped milk, one strawberry yoghurt and, tucked between, a folded copy of the *Scotsman*. But it was what was propped against the wall behind these daily rations that took the Duke's aristocratic breath away.

In a scrolled gilt frame stood a Raeburn portrait of a red-coated man with a romantic swath of plaid across his chest. He wore a fluffy white sporran, buckled pumps and tartan trews. One nonchalant hand rested on a tasselled sword hilt, the other held a black feathered bonnet. Behind him swirled an idealized Scottish landscape.

The man in the dressing gown picked up the picture with something approaching ecstasy. 'My God!' he cried. 'The third Duke's come home!'

And, still clutching the Raeburn to his breast, he danced a little jig of glee up and down his castle steps.

All over the world scenes of similar delight were played out, as Bennie Logan's 'borrowed' paintings were returned to their rightful owners.

And as Mrs Pargeter executed the unwritten contract to Veronica Chastaigne which she regarded as a point of honour.

Chapter Forty

Mrs Pargeter felt a warm glow of satisfaction as Gary's limousine delivered her and Hedgeclipper Clinton back to Greene's Hotel. The customized ambulance had been returned to its body shop underneath the arches, and she had left her uniform there. Hedgeclipper had removed his odious leisurewear and was once again dressed in sober black jacket and striped trousers. All the loose ends had been neatly tied together. Mrs Pargeter was of the opinion that the whole operation had been a very satisfactory day's work.

'Will you be dining in the hotel this evening?' asked Hedgeclipper, leading her across the foyer to the lift.

'Yes. On my own. Just a nice pampering meal. I feel I've deserved it.'

'You certainly have, Mrs Pargeter.'

'And thank you for all you did. I am so fortunate to be surrounded by people of such varied talents.'

'Think nothing of it.'

'There's a career for you in television if you ever decide to give this up.'

'Oh, I wouldn't dream of it, Mrs Pargeter. Greene's Hotel is my life,' said the manager as he opened the lift door for her.

'Well, I'm glad it is. I feel really comfortable here.'

'Excellent.' Hedgeclipper Clinton made a little bow to her. 'That is, after all, the aim of the exercise.'

Upstairs in her suite, Mrs Pargeter looked fondly at the photograph by her bedside. 'You know, my love, I think you'd have been quite proud of me today. We reproduced your old Chelmsford routine, and it worked a treat.' Seeming to read some reproach in the monochrome features, she went on, slightly defensively, 'I'm well aware that you never liked me to know anything about your work, but there was no other way this time. The paintings had to be returned. It was in a good cause, you see. You always had a lot of respect for Bennie Logan, and I'm sure you'd want his widow to be able to go to her grave in peace. And it isn't as if I was involved in anything criminal ...' She twisted her fingers, nervous under the photograph's scrutiny. 'Well, maybe at moments it kind of veered over towards the criminal ... I suppose technically, until the paintings were returned, we could have been said to be handling stolen goods. But that's the worst you could charge us with. Anyway, it's all done now. The job's complete and there's no evidence to link any of us with anything even mildly iffy.'

At that moment the telephone on the

bedside table rang. It was Hedgeclipper Clinton calling from downstairs, and there was a note of warning—almost of fear—in his voice. 'Mrs Pargeter, I wonder if you could come down. There are two gentlemen here who wish to speak to you on a very serious matter.'

'Oh really?' she said. 'Who are they?'

'They're Inspector Wilkinson and Sergeant Hughes,' said Hedgeclipper.

Chapter Forty-One

The faces of the two detectives were grim. Hedgeclipper Clinton too looked subdued. Mrs Pargeter could not help feeling a tremor of anxiety as she crossed the foyer to greet them.

'You haven't met Sergeant Hughes,' said Inspector Wilkinson.

'No, I haven't had the pleasure.' She extended a gracious hand to the young man. He transferred his briefcase to his left hand and gave hers a cold, formal shake. Under the grimness of his expression there was a disturbing glimmer of cocksure triumph.

'Hughes won't be staying with us.' Mrs Pargeter caught the spasm of annoyance these words sent across the Sergeant's face. 'You and I need to have a serious one-to-one talk, Mrs Pargeter.'

'Fine. Shall we go through to the bar?'

'I don't want to talk here. If you would be so good as to accompany me ...?'

It was phrased as a question, but left no doubt that it was really an order. Mrs Pargeter's unease grew. That word 'accompany' had overtones of too many television cop shows. 'I must ask you to accompany me to the station.' She had heard it spoken too often for comfort.

Mrs Pargeter didn't dare to imagine what had gone wrong. Had VVO's resolve finally cracked and had he shopped them all? Had Rod D'Acosta and his heavies said something to put the police on to her?

She felt rather stupid. Up until this point in her life, she had always religiously followed the instructions of the late Mr Pargeter. She had never been involved in anything that could be construed as criminal. She had had an unimpeachable record of innocence. But during the past weeks she'd got carried away. In the excitement of fulfilling Veronica Chastaigne's request and recreating the great Chelmsford operation, Mrs Pargeter had taken a much more hands-on role in the proceedings than she should have done. She had sacrificed the Olympian detachment which she had always previously maintained from the activities of her helpers. And now it looked as if she might be about to pay for her carelessness.

'Do you need to get a coat?' asked Inspector Wilkinson with formal solicitude.

'No, I'm fine. It's still very mild for September, isn't it?'

'Right, if you'd care to accompany us ...?' That word again. 'It's only a short drive.'

Sergeant Hughes hurried across to open the hotel's front door for her, and Mrs Pargeter moved elegantly and proudly across the foyer. As she passed a tense-faced Hedgeclipper Clinton, she gave an almost imperceptible flick of her eyebrow.

The instant the front door closed behind his guest and her police escort, Hedgeclipper was dialling Truffler Mason's number.

They didn't speak in the car. Hughes

267

drove, with Wilkinson sitting tensely beside him. In the back Mrs Pargeter gave a not entirely convincing display of nonchalance.

When the car stopped, she couldn't see a police station. They appeared to be in a street of shops and restaurants. But perhaps there was a hidden entrance to some official Metropolitan premises.

Mrs Pargeter tried to focus her mind on the plight in which she found herself. She knew what she had to do. The important thing was not to implicate anyone else. Mention no other names. She would just have to accept her own punishment, but see that she took no one else down with her.

Inspector Wilkinson said, 'Thank you, Hughes,' which the Sergeant reflected was out of character. Maybe his boss was trying to impress their suspect with his good manners. 'You can take the rest of the evening off.'

'I really think I should be with you, sir.'

'I *said* you can take the rest of the evening off.'

Hughes could not argue with the severity of the tone. 'All right, sir,' he conceded.

'And give me that dossier you've compiled.'

The Sergeant was about to remonstrate, but realized he couldn't. Inspector Wilkinson was in charge. If his boss ordered him to hand something across—even something as precious as the dossier he had spent so much time building up—then he had to do as he was told.

Silently, he opened his briefcase and handed over the folder.

'Thank you,' said Wilkinson again.

'I hope you'll be careful with it, sir. It's the only copy that—'

'Hughes, I have very considerable experience of handling highly sensitive evidence.'

'Yes, sir,' the Sergeant apologized.

'Rather more experience—if I may be forgiven for pointing it out—than you have.'

'Yes, sir.'

'So I can assure you that this document will be absolutely safe in my hands.' Hughes had no alternative but to nod acceptance of this.

Wilkinson got out of the car and opened the back door for Mrs Pargeter. 'If you would accompany me, please ...'

That word yet again. In trepidation she got out and stood awkwardly on the pavement. It was nearly dark now.

Inspector Wilkinson tapped the roof of the car and Sergeant Hughes, invisibly seething, drove off.

There was an uncomfortable silence as they stood, looking at each other. Mrs Pargeter didn't know where they were meant to be going, and for a moment the Inspector seemed uncertain too. Then he said abruptly, 'I thought we could have something to eat while we talked.'

'Fine,' she said, surprised.

Without ceremony, he led the way into a rather shabby little restaurant. Its origins were ultimately Greek, but it was the kind of place whose menu would feature 'English Dishes' alongside the range of kebabs. One wall was painted with a grubby Mediterranean seaside scene. Bottles and decorated plates hung on the walls, tangled in with dusty plastic vines and dully glowing Christmas lights.

A restaurant of this kind wasn't really Mrs Pargeter's gastronomic style. In spite of the predicament she was in, she couldn't help thinking of the menu at Greene's Hotel and the dinner she had been promising herself. She wondered rather gloomily how long it would be before she could next enjoy that kind of pampering.

There was nobody else inside the restaurant, except for a surly man with three days of five o'clock shadow. He acted as waiter, and possibly owner, and probably cook. He seemed to know Inspector Wilkinson, however, and grunted some kind of greeting as he led them across to a table with a printed plastic cover. Its surface felt slightly sticky as Mrs Pargeter eased her bulk into a bench seat against the wall.

The waiter/owner/cook dumped two plastic menus down on the table and shuffled off through a lopsided beaded curtain into the kitchen.

'Do you normally come here to conduct interrogations?' asked Mrs Pargeter, trying to ease the atmosphere that was beginning to loom between them.

'No,' Wilkinson replied shortly. 'Only when it's special.'

'Oh, right.' Mrs Pargeter took in her surroundings, and wondered how many hardened criminals those dingy walls had witnessed cracking under Inspector Wilkinson's relentless questioning.

Sergeant Hughes's folder lay unopened on the table in front of him, and he still seemed disinclined to commence the actual grilling. Mrs Pargeter was finding the delay stressful. Now she'd got this far, she wanted to get the whole thing over with as soon as possible. It wasn't going to be pleasant, but at least it could be quick.

She joined her plump hands together on the sticky plastic in front of her, and looked straight into the Inspector's eyes. He seemed thrown by this intense scrutiny, and chewed a corner of his moustache. His hands fiddled with a packet of cigarettes, taking one out to light up.

'Right,' said Mrs Pargeter. 'What is it you want to say to me?'

'Well ... The fact is ... I ...' For some reason Wilkinson was finding what he had to say difficult. And when he did say it, she could understand exactly why. 'The fact is, Mrs Pargeter, I've fallen in love with you.'

Chapter Forty-Two

Mrs Pargeter was so flabbergasted that she couldn't speak. This unfortunately gave Detective Inspector Craig Wilkinson the opportunity to expand on his passion.

'From the first moment I saw you, I

272

knew you were the woman for me. I can't pretend my life has been a great success. Professionally, I've been unlucky. I should have gone a lot further in the Police Force, but circumstances have been against me. A couple of times I got close to pulling off major coups, but on each occasion something went wrong.

'And in my private life, I haven't had much to write home about either. I was married, but that fell apart. Difficult profession, being a detective, if you want to keep a marriage going. Since then there have been a few other affairs—relationships, I suppose you could call them, though both words make them sound rather longer-lasting than they were.

'But since I've met you, Mrs Pargeter, I know why my previous encounters with women didn't work. I wasn't in love, you see. Now I know what love is. It's confusing, and wonderful, and stressful, and all-consuming. You obsess me. I have to keep seeing you. That's why I've kept popping up in your life with such frequency over the last few weeks. After the first time we met, I pretended it was for professional reasons, but in fact it was just because I needed to see you.'

Had I known that at the time, thought Mrs Pargeter, it could have saved me a considerable amount of anxiety. She opened her mouth to speak, but Craig Wilkinson wasn't finished yet.

'You are what I've been looking for all my life. I always knew I was going to make my mark one way or another. For a long time, I thought it would be as a detective. I thought I'd pull off the one big operation that ensured I was remembered for ever. But to have the one great relationship would be equally satisfactory. Then my life would not have been wasted.

'And don't worry about money, Mrs Pargeter. I'm reasonably well paid now, and will soon be receiving a decent pension. I don't have to pay any maintenance to my former wife, because she's living with someone else. We could have a very nice lifestyle.' He gestured expansively around the grubby restaurant. 'We could eat out at this kind of level every night of the week if we wanted to.

'And there are no logistical problems. We're both free. I'm divorced, you're a widow. There's nothing to stop us following the dictates of our hearts.

'So, go on, Mrs Pargeter, put me out of

my misery. Tell me—will you marry me?'

'You ready to order now?' Unseen by the Inspector, the waiter/owner/cook had lumbered up behind him and broken the moment.

'No!' Wilkinson snapped. The ash, which had been accumulating at the end of his cigarette throughout his long oration, now dropped on to the sticky plastic tablecloth.

'Give us another five minutes, if you would,' said Mrs Pargeter, more politely.

Grumbling in some foreign tongue, the waiter/owner/cook shambled back behind his beaded curtain.

'So, come on—what do you say, Mrs Pargeter?' The Inspector smiled what he deemed to be a sexy smile. 'Incidentally, given the circumstances, it does seem very formal for me to keep calling you "Mrs Pargeter".' Your first name's Melita, isn't it?'

'Yes,' she replied. 'It is. But very few people use it.' In fact the only person who'd really used it had been the late Mr Pargeter. It was a private thing between the two of them. She certainly didn't want someone like Inspector Wilkinson using the name.

'Ah. Anyway, I've had my say. You know where I stand.'

'I certainly do.'

'So then—what's your answer?'

He beamed at her confidently. The awful realization hit Mrs Pargeter that Craig Wilkinson had not considered the possibility of her refusal. He had become so caught up in his own interpretation of the scenario that he had taken her positive response for granted.

She decided to play for time, while she worked out the most tactful way of letting him down gently. 'Well, Inspector—' she smiled, 'Craig ... you must give me a minute or two to gather myself together. What you've just said has come as rather a surprise to me.'

'Not really?' He seemed genuinely puzzled. 'Surely you must have felt the electricity between us from the moment we first met?'

'Well ...' Mrs Pargeter replied discreetly. 'Not immediately, no.'

'Oh.' He looked surprised rather than disappointed, concluding perhaps that women were just slower than men at recognizing their destiny.

'There were a couple of things you said,

Craig, about your professional career ...?'

'Yes?'

'Two occasions when you got very close to pulling off coups, but something went wrong ...?'

He nodded, immediately blushing at the recollection.

'Could you tell me a bit about them?'

Wilkinson grimaced. 'I wouldn't normally talk to anyone about this, but, given the situation between us ...' (Mrs Pargeter decided it would be prudent to get the information before defining too precisely what the situation between them was.) 'I'll tell you.' He lit a new cigarette from the stub of the old one and ground out the butt on his side plate. 'Both of the incidents concerned a gentleman called Mr Pargeter ...'

'Oh, really?' She smiled innocently.

'Yes.' Wilkinson again acknowledged the coincidence. 'Same surname as you've got.'

'Mmm.'

'But, as we've established, nothing to do with you.'

'Oh, no.'

'Your late husband was a reputable businessman.'

'Oh, yes.'

'Well, on both occasions I was acting on a tip-off, and—'

'Excuse me, who would that tip-off have been from?'

'It was a regular copper's nark. Informer who went under the name of Posey Narker.'

'And did you meet him face to face?'

'No, there was just a phone number we rang, and his payment went into a secret bank account.'

'Right,' said Mrs Pargeter thoughtfully.

'So, anyway, the first incident happened in—' Inspector Wilkinson shuddered— 'Chelmsford.'

'Oh?'

'I was duped, led up the garden path—'—He bowed his head—'even made to look a fool.'

'Dear me.'

'I don't want to go into too much detail, but basically I ended up arranging a police escort to the docks at Dover for what I believed to be an ambulance, but was in fact a van containing a gang of villains and a huge haul of used fivers.'

'Bad luck,' Mrs Pargeter murmured, and then let out a little cough, almost as if she were trying to suppress some other sound.

'Yes, it was. Very unfortunate. Kind of thing it takes a long time to live down in the Police Force.'

'I can imagine.'

'What was really strange about it ...' the Inspector went on thoughtfully, 'was that only today, I got involved in another case which bore distinct similarities to the Chelmsford operation.'

'How very odd,' said Mrs Pargeter, all wide-eyed interest. 'You said there was a second occasion when you had rather bad luck ...?'

'Yes. This was again acting on a tip-off ...'

'From Posey Narker?'

Wilkinson nodded. 'This time I would have got the whole gang. Mr Pargeter was planning a really big raid on a Hatton Garden jewellers. It was going to involve every single person who'd ever worked for him. I could have arrested the lot of them. Whole thing was set up, I'd made detailed plans to entrap them, and ...'

'And what?' asked Mrs Pargeter, knowing the answer.

'And the raid never happened. Mr Pargeter died just before they were due to start.'

'Ah.' She looked a trifle misty-eyed. 'I see.'

'Anyway ...' Craig Wilkinson shook himself out of his retrospective mood. 'That's all in the past. So far as I'm concerned, all failure is in the past. Because now I have you. And together we can ensure that everything in the rest of our lives is successful.'

'Ye-es.' Mrs Pargeter began cautiously. 'When you say "now you have me" ...'

'Sorry.' The Inspector chuckled. 'Jumping the gun a bit there perhaps. Yes, we should get the formalities out of the way first, shouldn't we? Right, here's the official proposal. Do you want me to go down on my knees?'

'Certainly not. Not on this carpet.'

'Right.' He looked straight into the violet-blue eyes. 'Mrs Pargeter, will you marry me?'

'Oh ...' Looking at him with an expression that mingled pity, anguish and confusion, and lying through her teeth, she replied, 'That's one of the most difficult questions I've ever had to answer. You're a fine man, Craig ...'

'I know.' He nodded complacently. 'You said that once before.'

'Did I?'

'Yes. When we met for that drink in Greene's Hotel. You told me that I belonged to a fine body of men, and that I was a fine man myself ...'

'Yes?'

'... and that was the first time I realized that you felt the same way about me as I did about you.'

'Ah. Erm, Craig ... Yes, yes, you are a fine man, and—' she lied again, 'there are women all over the world who would give their eye-teeth to have an offer like the one you've just made to me ...'

He nodded, stroking the line of his moustache with satisfaction.

'... and I really wish that I could say yes to your proposal ...'

'You can. It's easy. Just say it.'

'I'm sorry. I can't.'

'Why ever not?'

'Because I'm in love with someone else.'

'What?' Inspector Wilkinson looked as if he'd been punched in the face. 'Then I'll go and meet this "someone else" face to face and I'll—'

'No. No, Craig, you can't,' she said gently. 'No one can meet him face to face. You see, he's dead.'

'Oh.'

'I'm sorry.' And Mrs Pargeter moved away from lies to the complete truth, as she went on, 'I'm talking about my late husband. He was a wonderful man. We loved each other and had a perfect marriage. And, though sometimes it almost annoys me, the fact remains that I can never love another man. There was only ever going to be one love in my life. I've been fortunate enough to have had that, to have enjoyed it for many years, and I know it can never happen again.'

There was moisture in Mrs Pargeter's eyes, and it caught a reflected gleam in Craig Wilkinson's. 'I see,' he said flatly. 'Well, that's it really, isn't it?'

'I'm afraid it is.'

'Your husband, Mrs Pargeter, was a very lucky man.' She nodded. 'And he must have been a very good man, to inspire such devotion.'

'He was,' she agreed. 'He was a very good man indeed.'

Wilkinson nodded ruefully. 'So you will never be mine. That's not going to be the way I make my mark on the world.'

'No. I'm afraid it isn't. Still,' she said encouragingly, 'maybe things'll pick up in your professional life.'

Inspector Wilkinson let out a hollow laugh. 'Yes, I can just see it. No,' he continued, cast down in gloom, 'some people are destined to pass through life without making any mark at all, and I'm afraid I'm one of them.'

'Oh ...' said Mrs Pargeter, trying desperately to think of something that could ease the awkwardness of the situation.

A sound like a choke emerged from Craig Wilkinson's mouth, and she realized to her horror that he was fighting back tears. And he wasn't of the generation who would allow themselves to be seen crying by a woman. He rose to his feet.

'I must go,' he announced abruptly, and walked out of the restaurant.

Leaving his folder on the table in front of him.

Mrs Pargeter reached across casually and picked it up.

The waiter/owner/cook, alerted by the sound of the door closing, emerged from the dark recesses of his kitchen. 'Are you ready to order now?' he grunted.

'No,' said Mrs Pargeter, extricating herself from her bench seat. 'I don't think

I'd ever be ready to order in a restaurant like this, thank you very much.'

And, clutching Sergeant Hughes's folder to her ample bosom, she walked out. Thank goodness there was still time for her to get a decent, pampering dinner at Greene's Hotel.

Chapter Forty-Three

'Who'd you say had compiled this little lot?' asked Truffler Mason, when he'd finished reading the contents of the folder.

'His name's Sergeant Hughes. He's been working with Inspector Wilkinson.'

The private investigator nodded. 'Well, he's a bright boy. Far too bright a boy to be working in the Police Force. If they start recruiting many more people of this calibre, there's going to be a whole lot of nice, smooth-running apple-carts upset.'

They were sitting in the Greene's Hotel bar. Mrs Pargeter had summoned Truffler as soon as she got back to her suite, but he hadn't arrived until after she'd finished her dinner (delicious, the perfect therapy

284

after the rather melodramatic encounter she'd just experienced). Truffler made do with smoked salmon sandwiches, and it seemed silly for them not to be sharing a postprandial bottle of champagne. So that's what they were doing.

Mrs Pargeter had flicked through the contents of the folder, and immediately decided it needed more expert scrutiny, which was why she'd called Truffler.

'No,' he went on, 'so long as we're dealing with dumbos like Craggy Wilkinson, we don't have a problem. He'd get the wrong end of the stick in a relay race.'

'Yes,' Mrs Pargeter agreed with feeling.

'But Sergeant Hughes is clearly something else.' Truffler shook the sheaf of papers in his hand. 'This stuff's dynamite. Got to see that it's suppressed somehow. I mean, this could do a lot of harm to a lot of people.'

'There were rather too many familiar names in there, weren't there?'

'Yes.' Truffler looked aggrieved. 'And it's not as if any of them're villains. All been going absolutely straight since your husband died. All good, upright citizens doing their bit for society. No, it'd be a tragedy if any of these blokes got hassle about stuff that happened such a long time ago. A real tragedy.'

'I agree. So what're we going to do about it? Can Jukebox Jarvis get into the police computer again and make a few changes?'

'That may be the answer ... so long as the boy wonder actually did this on the office computer. If he did it on a personal laptop or something, then we may have to get Keyhole Crabbe to pay a visit to wherever he lives.'

'It'll be all right, won't it?' asked Mrs Pargeter anxiously.

'Course it'll be all right. Best thing we've got going for us is still the fact that old Craggy Wilkinson's in charge of the case. Unless he's undergone a total character transplant, he's not going to like having some smart-arse Sergeant as a sidekick. Like all deeply stupid people, there's nothing he hates more than dealing with someone who's intelligent. I think there's a very strong chance that Wilkinson'll suppress this entire dossier without us having to do a thing.'

'It would be wonderful if that happened, wouldn't it?'

'Yes, it would, Mrs P. In the meantime there are other things we can do by way of damage limitation.'

'Good.' Mrs Pargeter grinned. 'And of course there was some information in the folder we didn't know, did we?'

'That is very true.'

'Particularly about Posey Narker. Information on the informant.'

'Right,' said Truffler grimly. 'Glad we've finally got him identified.'

'Very interesting, wasn't it? And it makes sense of quite a few odd details. Clarifies the Rod D'Acosta connection at least.'

'And the connection with the other gentleman,' said Truffler. He looked at his watch. 'I asked Gary to bring the car round at ten. That is, if you don't mind another trip out, Mrs P ...?'

'Mind? Of course I don't mind. I wouldn't want to miss this bit, Truffler.'

Gary's limousine waited outside the exclusive mansion block, while Mrs Pargeter and Truffler Mason approached the tall portico and pressed the entry-phone button.

'Yes?' Even through the crackle from the small speaker, the voice was easily identifiable.

'Mr Chastaigne, my name is Mrs Pargeter.'

'I don't think I know you,' Toby Chastaigne's voice crackled back.

'No, I don't think you do. But I want to talk to you about Rod D'Acosta.'

Toby Chastaigne's pudgy face looked tense and drawn while he closed the sliding grille. As the lift jolted into action, his eyes avoided those of his visitors.

'The fact is,' said Mrs Pargeter easily, 'the police are holding Mr D'Acosta and his merry men ...'

'What's that to me?'

'Well, I was just thinking that the D'Acosta gang might well be prepared to talk about who their paymaster was ...'

'I still don't understand what you're getting at.'

The lift stopped at the second floor. Toby Chastaigne opened the double grilles and led Mrs Pargeter and Truffler to the front door of his flat.

'What I'm getting at,' Mrs Pargeter continued evenly, 'is the fact that I believe you were behind the theft of the paintings from Chastaigne Varleigh.'

'That's nonsense,' Toby Chastaigne

snorted, reaching into his pocket for keys. 'I disapproved of my mother having them in the first place.'

'I think you were intending to sell them illegally and take the profits.'

'But I wouldn't begin to know how to sell paintings illegally.'

As he spoke, Toby Chastaigne pushed open the front door and ushered them into his flat. Mrs Pargeter looked around with interest. The charcoal-grey walls and the uncomfortable-looking metal furniture were informatively familiar.

'No,' she said, looking straight into the flat-owner's eyes, 'I agree you wouldn't know how to sell them yourself. But I think you know someone who could do it for you.'

Chapter Forty-Four

Mrs Pargeter and Truffler sat in the back, as the limousine eased away from the mansion block where Toby Chastaigne lived.

'I'm sorry,' said the private investigator.

'I should've been on to Palings sooner.'

'It doesn't matter.' Mrs Pargeter looked thoughtful as other bits of the jigsaw slotted into place. 'It explains why the D'Acosta boys moved in on the paintings when they did, though. Palings must've tipped them off about our plans.'

'Yes.' Truffler joined in the piecing-together. 'And it was him who encouraged you to send VVO as courier.'

'Trying to put another spanner in our works, hmm. I still feel stupid about that. Behaved like a real softie there. No, Palings took advantage of me.'

'Not only of you, Mrs P,' said Truffler grimly. 'He took advantage of your husband and all.'

'Yes.'

'If he was Posey Narker from the start ... it doesn't bear thinking of, the number of operations he nearly ruined. We all thought it was strange the way the cops kept second-guessing us. No, we was lucky. But for the fact that old Craggy Wilkinson was in charge in most of the cases, we could have had real problems. Any DI who wasn't one carnation short of a bouquet would have done for the lot of us. Palings Price has got a lot to answer for.'

There was a silence, before, with his large hands tensed on his thighs and a shadow of menace in his voice, Truffler Mason asked, 'What do you want done about him?'

'Palings?'

He nodded. 'He's been a naughty boy, and naughty boys have to be punished.'

'Oh,' said Mrs Pargeter airily, 'for the time being, I think we can leave that to the police. The D'Acosta boys will put them on to Toby, and Toby's bound to implicate Palings. So he'll soon be safely in custody.'

The huge hands on Truffler's thighs relaxed. 'You're a very forgiving woman, Mrs Pargeter.'

'No, Truffler,' she corrected him piously. 'Just a good citizen who has great faith in the British legal system.'

And Mrs Pargeter smiled serenely.

But the private investigator had caught another undercurrent in her tone. 'You said "for the time being" Palings could be left to the police ...'

'Yes.'

'Meaning that you might have other plans for dealing with him later ...?'

'Meaning exactly that, Truffler, yes.'

'Can't tell me what, can you?'

She gave an apologetic shake of the head. 'Sorry. Not quite yet. I'm still just working out the details.'

Gary's limousine, as ever having a charmed life so far as traffic wardens were concerned, was parked on the double yellow lines directly outside the law courts, so the chauffeur had a perfect view of the happy scene that unfolded before him.

VVO emerged first, with an ecstatic Deirdre Winthrop hugging him. In honour of his court appearance, the painter was dressed in a sedate grey suit and sober tie. There was no sign of his trademark beret, and there wasn't even paint under his fingernails.

The happy couple were followed out by an equally delighted Mrs Pargeter, escorted by Jukebox Jarvis and an enormously fat man in a pin-striped suit, whose huge body tapered down to tiny black shoes. He was Arnold Justiman, one of the most eminent barristers of his generation, whose services had been frequently called on by the late Mr Pargeter. Arnold Justiman's record for ironing out the misunderstandings which had led to his clients being falsely accused was so impressive that it was said he could have got Vlad the Impaler off with a caution.

For a man of his skills, ensuring the dropping of all the charges against Reg Winthrop—a.k.a Vincent Vin Ordinaire—had been an intellectual fleabite, but that didn't make Mrs Pargeter any the less grateful for his efforts. 'Well done, Arnold,' she enthused.

'Not very difficult,' he said modestly. 'With all the other paintings having been returned, there wasn't much of a case against him. Now the two Madonnas and the Rubens nude will be returned to their rightful owners in the normal way.'

'And neither Bennie Logan nor Veronica Chastaigne's names will ever be mentioned in connection with them.'

'Good heavens, no.' He was shocked even at the idea.

'Anyway, many thanks. And full marks for keeping it out of the papers.'

Arnold Justiman shrugged and smiled a smile of patrician confidence. 'Most things can be arranged if you know the right people.'

'Yes,' Mrs Pargeter agreed. 'I've always found that.' She looked at her watch.

'And now we'd better go and pay our other call.'

The barrister nodded.

'I'll just say goodbye.' She moved across to the group celebrating the painter's acquittal and shook him firmly by the hand. 'Congratulations, VVO—marvellous news!'

He clasped her hand in both of his. 'Can't thank you enough, Mrs Pargeter.'

'No, nor can I,' said Deirdre. 'I mean, what it must have cost to get Mr Justiman to—'

Mrs Pargeter raised a hand to stop her and beamed beatifically. 'It was my pleasure.'

'Well, you're a saint, Mrs Pargeter, a real saint.'

At that moment Truffler Mason emerged from the law courts. His long arms were wrapped around the three VVO originals which had covered the valuable paintings in the Winthrops' abortive smuggling expedition. 'Here, these exhibits were released for you, VVO,' he called across.

'Oh, terrific!' cried the genius, delighted to be reunited with his masterworks. He gazed fondly at the top painting, the pink-bowed lamb frolicking in front of its winsome windmill.

But the effect of the picture on its creator was as nothing to the impact it had on Jukebox Jarvis. The archivist's jaw fell open; he was transfixed by the canvas in front of him. 'Hey, who did this?' he asked in an awestruck voice. 'Can I see the others?'

'Sure.' VVO revealed the lovable ducklings on the frozen pond and then, with a dramatic flourish, the Scottie dog and the fluffy white cat. He looked into Jukebox Jarvis's mesmerized face. 'Do you like them?'

The archivist replied in a voice low with reverence. 'Like them? I think they're absolutely wonderful. I may not know much about art, but by golly I know what I like.' He looked plaintively at the artist, not daring to hope. 'They're not for sale, by any chance, are they ...?'

'Well,' replied VVO, unable to disguise how delighted he was by the question, 'since you ask ...'

As the artist began to expatiate to his new fan on his art, his struggles, his intentions, his ambitions, Mrs Pargeter grinned across at Truffler Mason. Together with Arnold Justiman, they moved across to get into Gary's limousine.

Chapter Forty-Five

Since they had last visited her, Veronica Chastaigne seemed to have shrunk even further. Her body looked lost amidst the bedclothes, her skin tighter, her tiny bones more prominent. Had she been able to stand up, a breath of wind could have blown her away. Only the fierce sparkle in her eye showed the indomitable will which was keeping her alive until all her earthly business had been discharged to her satisfaction.

Arnold Justiman, looking even bigger looming over the birdlike figure in the hospital bed, had taken her through the provisions of the new will. As Mrs Pargeter and Truffler Mason looked on, he proffered a fountain pen to the invalid and pointed to the relevant line on the document.

'So if you could just sign there, Mrs Chastaigne ... assuming, that is, you're happy with the provisions ...'

Her voice was very feeble as she said, 'I'm delighted with them,' but the signature that she affixed to the will was firm and definite.

The barrister turned to Mrs Pargeter and Truffler. 'And if you two could just sign as witnesses ...?'

'Melita Pargeter' was appended in Mrs Pargeter's round, almost childish, hand, and as she passed the document across to Truffler, she said, 'It'll be nice for you to know that the National Trust's looking after Chastaigne Varleigh, won't it, Veronica?'

The response from the fading figure in the bed was surprisingly robust. 'It'll be even nicer to know that Toby's getting absolutely nothing from me! Serve him right for trying to disclaim his own father.' She chuckled breathily. 'Toby always insisted he wanted to stand on his own two feet. Well, now he can see what it feels like.'

A peaceful smile stole across her lined face. 'And now I know the paintings are back where they belong ... there's nothing left to worry me.'

Arnold Justiman took the will from Truffler Mason and folded it neatly into an envelope. 'So ... all done.'

'Yes. By me, Veronica Chastaigne ...'

'... being of sound mind ...' Mrs Pargeter supplied.

'Absolutely,' the old lady agreed. 'No problems there. It's only this wretched body that's giving out. Oh well, never mind. It's not as if I haven't had a good run for other people's money ...'

And she chuckled wheezily, but merrily, at the thought.

Now it was just the two women in the private room. 'I asked you to stay,' Veronica Chastaigne murmured, 'because there is one more thing ...'

'Yes?' said Mrs Pargeter. 'You tell me. Whatever it is, I'll see that it gets done. It's a point of honour with me to sort out all my late husband's unfinished business.'

'It's about Toby.' A hard look came into the old lady's eyes. 'I still don't think Toby's suffered enough.'

'Well, he hasn't really suffered at all yet. He doesn't even know Chastaigne Varleigh's going to the National Trust. But don't worry, I think he will suffer,' Mrs Pargeter reassured her. 'The people who actually stole the paintings from the Long Gallery are in police custody. They're bound to implicate Palings Price—that's

Denzil Price, the interior designer—and then I'm sure he'll shop your son.'

'And what will Toby be charged with?'

'I don't know what the technical expression will be—"aiding and abetting a robbery" perhaps? I mean, he must've given the information to the thieves about the secret hoard at Chastaigne Varleigh. Or perhaps it'll be "handling stolen goods" ...'

'And you think he'll get a custodial sentence?' asked the old lady eagerly.

'I would imagine so. Depends as ever, of course, on the kind of legal representation he gets. As Arnold Justiman would tell you, the right lawyer can get anyone off anything.'

'Yes.' Veronica Chastaigne shook her head thoughtfully. 'No, I want something more watertight than that.'

'Sorry? What do you mean?'

'I mean that I want to ensure Toby goes to prison for a long, long time.' Mrs Pargeter was taken aback by the venom with which these words were spoken. A fanatical light blazed in the pale eyes, as Veronica Chastaigne went on, 'What he was trying to do was a complete betrayal of me—and, even worse, of his father. Having spent his whole life disapproving and being sniffy about Bennie's career, and having claimed he wanted nothing to do with the paintings in the Long Gallery, Toby was actually proposing to get them sold on the black market. He was intending to profit from the very business he claimed always to have despised. I've never had a problem with good, honest criminality, but if there's one thing I cannot tolerate it's hypocrisy!'

'Yes,' Mrs Pargeter agreed. 'I'm with you on that one.'

'So I don't want Toby to get away with it. I want to ensure that he gets punished for what he's done.'

Mrs Pargeter grimaced. 'The trouble is, he hasn't done that much. He undoubtedly intended to sell off the paintings, but since they were returned to their rightful owners before the selling process could be started, he never got round to that part of the crime.'

'No,' Veronica Chastaigne's mouth twitched angrily from side to side. It was amazing the intensity of seething that could fit into such a tiny body. 'Well, that's what I want you to do something about, Mrs Pargeter,' she said finally.

'Sorry? What exactly?'

'I want you to ensure that my son Toby goes to prison for a long, long time.'

'On what charge?'

'I've told you—hypocrisy!'

'Mmm ...' said Mrs Pargeter tentatively. 'Although I'm fully in agreement with you that hypocrisy is a despicable crime, I don't think you'll find that in the British system of justice—'

'I'm not talking about justice!' the old lady snapped. 'I'm talking about what's right!'

'Ah. Well, those are two very different things,' Mrs Pargeter agreed.

'And which do you believe to be the more important?'

'What's right, obviously.'

'Exactly!' There was a gleam of triumph in the faded eyes. 'So I want you to arrange that what's right gets done. I want Toby to go to prison for a long time to pay for his crimes.'

'Even the ones he didn't technically commit?'

'Yes! Particularly the ones he didn't technically commit!' She looked pleadingly across at the younger woman. 'Could you do that for me?'

Mrs Pargeter smiled comfortably. What she was being asked to do did fit in rather well with a plan that was already formulating in her mind. 'Yes, Veronica. I can do that for you. No problem.'

As she left the hospital, thinking back to the display of mother love she'd just witnessed, Mrs Pargeter decided it was probably just as well she'd never had children.

Chapter Forty-Six

Once she had decided what needed doing, it was all done very quickly.

Immediately after her visit to the hospital, Mrs Pargeter convened a meeting with Truffler Mason and Hamish Ramon Henriques, and spelled out her plans to them. They were in complete agreement with what she proposed.

Their first port of call was the little terraced house where Jukebox Jarvis lived. He immediately accessed the police computer system (that day's six-letter codeword was 'peeler', an inventive historical variation), and discovered that Sergeant Hughes had not used an office machine on which to compile his dossier.

This was only a minor setback, and indeed one that they had been anticipating. While still inside the police computer system, Jukebox Jarvis found Sergeant Hughes's home address, and was also able to confirm from the duty rosters that the young man was at work all that day.

Keyhole Crabbe, the late Mr Pargeter's most trusted security expert, had been alerted to a possible call-out, and was immediately summoned from his home in Bedford. Accompanied by Jukebox Jarvis, he went to Sergeant Hughes's flat, where the double locks and burglar alarm proved only a momentary obstacle. Once inside, Jukebox quickly found the Sergeant's laptop, located the file from which his dossier had been printed, and deleted the entire contents of that and its back-up. He resisted the temptation to leave a cheeky message.

All that remained to be done then was for Mrs Pargeter and Truffler Mason to concoct an alternative dossier on the alleged criminal activities of the late Mr

Pargeter and his associates.

It was a work of great simplicity, but, in the view of its creators, considerable beauty.

Sergeant Hughes had done well in his researches. He was a gifted detective, who might well have lived up to his first name of Hercule, had not the jealousy of crusty old superiors like Inspector Wilkinson (and a little finessing by associates of Mrs Pargeter) held back his career.

Hughes had made the link between Chastaigne Varleigh and the series of international art thefts initiated by Bennie Logan. He had identified the role of Palings Price in these crimes and the interior designer's current association with Toby Chastaigne.

More disturbingly, he had traced the links from Bennie Logan and Palings Price back to the late Mr Pargeter. Once that connection had been made, a whole set of new names became ripe for investigation. By going back into the old files from the period immediately before Mr Pargeter's death, when Inspector Wilkinson had been getting close to arresting the whole gang, Hughes had named Truffler Mason, Hedgeclipper Clinton, Hamish

Ramon Henriques, Keyhole Crabbe and Gary the chauffeur.

Truffler had not been guilty of hyperbole when he described the contents of the dossier as dynamite.

Still, the original had now been deleted from the Sergeant's laptop. All that remained was to ensure that it was never reconstructed in the same form, and that Sergeant Hughes was discreetly removed from the scene.

It was to achieve this first aim that Mrs Pargeter and Truffler Mason compiled their revised dossier. The document did not attempt to excise all reference to the late Mr Pargeter. It was more subtle than that. As in Sergeant Hughes's researches, links were traced between the dead man and a series of associates. It was in the names of these associates that the new dossier diverged from the original.

Rod D'Acosta was implicated in a series of the late Mr Pargeter's operations. So were his acolytes, the heavies called Ray, Phil and Sid. Their involvement was at a strictly Rent-A-Muscle level, so their sentences would not be as long as those handed down to the ringleaders.

And these ringleaders were of course

identified in the new dossier. The master-mind behind a great many vicious crimes turned out to be Denzil—known in the underworld as 'Palings'—Price. And, interestingly, he had for a long time been in cahoots with a gentleman called Toby Chastaigne.

The criminal network run by these two was extensive, but, sadly from the police point of view, all of the other major players in their gang had since died. (Compiling this list of names had been Truffler Mason's task, which he had completed with his customary efficiency. In fact, it had been easy. In the dusty chaos of his office, he kept all the back numbers of a magazine called *Inside Out*. Known affectionately in the underworld as 'The Lag Mag', this publication noted the comings and goings, releases and transfers of the country's prison population. All Truffler had to do was to consult the 'Obituary' sections, and he soon had an extensive list of safely dead villains.)

The men named in the new dossier formed the core of a gang responsible for some of the most audacious criminal operations of the previous two decades, and unanswerable evidence was provided against all of them. Bringing to justice the six who were still alive would neatly tie a bow on a long series of unsolved crimes. Once they were put away, the police file on the late Mr Pargeter could be closed for ever.

The dossier took a couple of days to get right, but, when finished, it was, though Mrs Pargeter said it herself, a beautiful piece of work. She did have a momentary pang of conscience contemplating the length of the jail sentences the named men were likely to get, but then she remembered Veronica Chastaigne's important distinction between the concepts of 'justice' and of 'what's right'. Mrs Pargeter then felt absolved from any possible blame about what she was doing.

All that remained was for Jukebox Jarvis to access the police computer once again to add a couple of refinements. This he did with no problem (invention having run out, they were back to using 'copper' as that day's six-letter password).

Once inside the system, Jukebox followed Mrs Pargeter's instructions. The text of the new dossier was copied into a secret file in the computer which sat on the desk of

Inspector Craig Wilkinson.

And then there was the small matter of Sergeant Hughes ... Truffler Mason had suggested, very tentatively and obliquely, that this could be a job for Vanishing Vernon or even, remembering how he got his nickname, Hedgeclipper Clinton. But Mrs Pargeter was vehemently against the idea.

Her solution to the problem was much more ingenious. Obeying her instructions, Jukebox Jarvis accessed the files of the Met's personnel department.

A few relevant keystrokes were made, and the following Monday Sergeant Hughes started his new posting at a dog-handling unit in South Wales.

One piece of unfinished business remained. She wasn't obliged to do it, but for Mrs Pargeter it was a point of honour that she should once again speak face to face with Craig Wilkinson.

She announced herself at the station reception, and he was clearly surprised when she entered his office.

Mrs Pargeter spoke first to ease the potential embarrassment. 'The circumstances of our parting last time were so abrupt that I didn't want there to be any ill feeling between us.'

'No, no, of course not. I'm sorry. It's something that doesn't very often happen to me, but I just got the wrong end of the stick.' This wasn't a deliberate lie on the Inspector's part; he did just genuinely lack self-knowledge.

'The other thing was—'—Mrs Pargeter placed Sergeant Hughes's folder on the desk—'you left this behind in the restaurant. I've no idea what's in it—' (now that was a deliberate lie) 'but I'm sure it's important.'

'Well, yes, yes, it could be.' In spite of Sergeant Hughes's furious questions about where the dossier was, Wilkinson had been too deeply sunk in his own gloom to think much about it.

'Mind you, these days losing a copy of a document's not such a problem as it used to be. Presumably you have the text on your computer, don't you?'

'Er, well ...' The Inspector looked across at the alien keyboard and monitor on a small table on the other side of the room. Its layer of dust showed how often it got used. In Wilkinson's oft-stated, Luddite view, 'A good copper doesn't need computers. A good copper works by instinct and intuition.'

'Actually, in this case,' he went on, 'most of the research for that dossier was done by my junior, Sergeant Hughes.'

'But he'd probably have sent a copy to your computer, so that you could check it.'

'I'm not sure that he would. He's a rather secretive type, Hughes. Likes to keep things to himself.'

'Surely, though, when working with someone of your eminence and track record, Craig, he'd know that it was his duty to share everything with you.'

'Well, maybe ...'

'I bet you're just being modest. I bet there's a copy of his work on your computer, and you've added all kinds of refinements and clever bits to it.'

Inspector Wilkinson chuckled. 'I suppose you could be right.'

'I bet all the original thinking in there comes from you, not from Sergeant Hughes at all.'

He nodded modestly. 'Yes, it probably does.'

Mrs Pargeter had been right. She'd reckoned, in Inspector Wilkinson, she was up against one of those bosses who, whatever had been the provenance for a good idea, would always claim it as their own.

'Anyway,' she went on, 'I really just wanted to bring this back to you and, you know, say I'm sorry that we couldn't work anything out on ...' she blushed coyly '... the other business.'

'Think nothing of it, Mrs Pargeter. I've come to terms with the truth now. I am just destined to be a failure in my private life.'

'But—'—she tapped the dossier meaningfully—'destined to be a huge success in your professional life.'

He gave a self-depreciating shrug. 'Ooh, I don't know about that.'

'Well, I *do*,' Mrs Pargeter asserted. 'And what's more, I don't like you saying you're a failure in your private life ... at least not so far as I'm concerned. I told you—you're a very fine man. And,' she lied, 'I'm sure I could be very attracted to you, were it not for the fact ...'

'That you're still in love with one of the finest, most honest men who ever walked God's earth ...'

'I'm afraid that's it, yes.'

311

Wilkinson chuckled. '... even if he did share a surname with someone of rather less respectable reputation.'

Mrs Pargeter joined in the joke. Then she gathered herself together, preparatory to leaving. 'Well, I do hope we'll meet again, Craig.'

'Yes. Maybe finish that rather splendid dinner at my favourite restaurant that you never got round to the other night ...?'

She let out a gentle laugh. 'Ye-es. Or perhaps you'd like to come to Greene's Hotel instead.'

'One or the other, eh?'

'No,' she said firmly. 'Greene's Hotel.' She rose from her chair. 'Well, I must be off. You just concentrate on that very clever dossier you've worked out.'

Inspector Wilkinson nodded. 'I might just have another look at it, yes.' As she had known it would, the idea planted in his mind had grown, and he was now almost convinced that the dossier was all his own work.

'See you again soon, Craig,' said Mrs Pargeter as he led her to the door. She stopped to give him a gentle peck on the cheek. 'I'm just so sorry that it couldn't work out ... you know, you and me.'

'Yes, well ...' He shrugged manfully at the sadnesses of life. 'There you go.'

'Mmm.'

'And, incidentally, Mrs Pargeter, if there's ever anything I can do for you ... any information on police matters ... professional advice ... whatever ... even top-secret stuff ... well, you only have to ask.'

'Do you know, Craig ...' said Mrs Pargeter thoughtfully, 'I might just take you up on that.'

Chapter Forty-Seven

When she got back to Greene's Hotel, Mrs Pargeter looked contritely at the photograph on her bedside table. Though the black and white features of the soberly suited gentleman in the frame never actually changed, she could read different moods into the well-known face, and the mood she could see now was one of reproach. That expression had remained since their previous conversation had been interrupted by the arrival at the hotel of Inspector Wilkinson and Sergeant Hughes.

'I'm sorry,' said Mrs Pargeter to her dead husband. 'I did get a bit carried away, and I took risks I shouldn't have taken. You never wanted me to know anything about your working life, and that was a restriction I was happy to accept. But in the past weeks certain facts have been presented to me, which I know you wouldn't want me to know.

'Well, don't you worry about that at all. I will never mention any of those facts to another living soul. In fact, I will forget about them, totally erase them from my mind. It'll be as if I had never known those details about you. We'll go back to the relationship that we've always had.

'And in future,' she continued humbly, 'I will see that this kind of thing never happens again. I will never again pry into your business affairs. And, though I did maybe go a little bit too far this time, it was in a good cause. I know you'd have wanted me to fulfil your promise to Veronica Chastaigne.

'That's all I wanted to say, love. And to remind you, of course, how much I appreciate all you've done for me in the past, and all you manage to continue to do for me now. You know, what I said to Inspector Wilkinson was absolutely true. You are the love of my life. There will never be anyone else.'

Mrs Pargeter found there were tears in her eyes. She brushed them away, and when she looked back at the photograph of the late Mr Pargeter, she could see that the expression on his face had changed to one of forgiveness and deep, requited love.

Chapter Forty-Eight

The little parish church of Chastaigne Upton was much fuller than on the average Sunday, and on this particular Thursday it was not difficult to believe in the continuity of human existence. Supposedly there had been a church on the same site in Saxon times, and the Normans had replaced it with the grey stone building that still stood, defying the advance of progress. The green graveyard undulated with the contours of old tombs; its grassy surface was broken up by oddly angled stone crosses worn to smooth anonymity. Here indeed was a peaceful spot in which a body might sleep for all eternity, and which might inspire thoughts of an Overall Purpose or a Greater Power even in the most irreligious of breasts.

The congregation that had assembled in Chastaigne Upton was not a very religious one. Many had not been near a church since the funeral of the late Mr Pargeter, and for some the sole purpose of any visits before that occasion had been theft. But even in the most materialistic of bosoms something spiritual stirred that afternoon, as they looked at the plain light wood coffin and contemplated its imminent return to the earth, where it and its contents would slowly rot away, to become part of the eternal cycle of decay and regeneration.

Sunlight dappled the colours of the stained glass windows across the aisles. The air inside the church was heavy with the perfume of the many flowers that surrounded the coffin and added brightness to the occasion.

The silk print of Mrs Pargeter's dress was even brighter than the flowers. Following the express directive of the deceased, guests had been invited to 'dress cheerfully'; there was not a hint of black in the whole church.

As she looked along her pew, Mrs Pargeter felt a glow of satisfied pride. immediately next to her was Truffler Mason, next to him Gary, then Hamish Ramon Henriques and Hedgeclipper Clinton. In the row in front stood Kevin the doorman, Vanishing Vernon, Jukebox Jarvis, VVO and Deirdre. They were a good crew, thought Mrs Pargeter fondly. She really was very blessed in her friends. And very blessed in having shared her life with the late Mr Pargeter, who was responsible for building up such a reliable band of friends.

The one who had proved not to be reliable, Palings Price, a.k.a. Posey Narker, was not in the church. He was in Wandsworth, on remand along with the D'Acosta gang, all of whom were awaiting trial on a surprisingly long list of charges.

Sergeant Hughes wasn't present either. He was at that moment in a kennel outside Cardiff, trying unsuccessfully to bond with an Alsatian bitch called Geraldine.

'We are gathered here,' the vicar said, 'not just to mourn the death, but to celebrate the life of Veronica Chastaigne ... a wife who enjoyed the love and protection of a good man ... an art-lover who lived all her life surrounded by beautiful things. In honour of which, we will now sing Veronica Chastaigne's favourite hymn "All Things Bright and Beautiful".'

As the organ rumbled out its intro and hymn books were raised, Mrs Pargeter could not resist a sly look across the aisle to the pew on the other side. Toby Chastaigne wore an expression of considerable disgruntlement. And it wasn't only caused by the presence of Inspector Craig Wilkinson next to him. The bewildering list of charges that he and Palings Price faced had something to do with his mood as well.

The moment Wilkinson raised his hymn book, Toby lifted his hands too. He had little alternative. Handcuffs, by their very design, demand a degree of synchronization.

On Detective Inspector Craig Wilkinson's face was an expression of enormous satisfaction. The presentation of his dossier had been a stunning success. In spite of assertions from Sergeant Hughes that it was all nonsense and didn't tally with the facts, Wilkinson's Superintendent had been very impressed by his Inspector's detailed case study.

It was a pity that so many of the named villains had died before justice could catch up with them, but at least there were six surviving defendants to throw the book at. Wilkinson's unravelling of the complex connections in the network of criminals had been recognized as masterly. The Superintendent even apologized for having underestimated his long-serving officer in the past, and not recognizing the genius that lay beneath an apparently plodding exterior. He recommended Wilkinson for immediate promotion to the rank of chief inspector.

Most importantly, thanks to the exhaustive, tenacious work of one dedicated detective, the outstanding file on the late Mr Pargeter could be finally closed.

Oh yes, thought Wilkinson, running his tongue along the luxuriance of his curly moustache, I've certainly made my mark in the Police Force.

The hymn singing from the assembled congregation in the little church of Chastaigne Upton was full-bodied and surprisingly tuneful.

All things bright and beautiful,
All creatures great and small,
All things wise and wonderful,
The Lord God made them all.

And Mrs Pargeter, who didn't believe in God, thought indulgently that if it wasn't Him who'd made them, then it was someone else. And whoever it was had good reason to be proud of His or Her creation.